IVY'S FALL

LINDA WINSTEAD JONES

Cover design by Elizabeth Wallace
http://designwithin.carbonmade.com/

❀ Created with Vellum

CHAPTER 1

Ivy hated change with a passion, and these days that meant she was shit out of luck.

Mystic Springs was growing and changing day by day, bit by bit. Everyone but Ivy seemed to be happy about the shift, but then they were all getting married and having babies and starting new businesses. It was like life had been stalled, and now it was on the move again. For everyone but her.

There were only two empty spaces on Main Street, when not so long ago there had been more storefronts vacant than occupied. Fewer homes were for sale in her small town that was suddenly not quite as small as it had once been. *For Sale* signs had come down; lawns were mowed regularly. There was a sense of life that had been missing for a very long time, in the air and in the people all around her. For this school year, more kids had been enrolled in the K-12 school. She'd heard they'd had to hire two new teachers.

On occasion Ivy wondered if someone had managed to cast a spell on the sly, but all indications were that this was a completely natural shift in the makeup and atmosphere of the town. Natural. Bah!

Her twin, Eve, was not only married and disgustingly happy, but newly pregnant.

Quite a few Springers who'd moved away over the last several years had come back. Returnees included a candy maker, one of the new teachers, and a doctor, as well as a couple of retirees. Elaine Forrester's niece Molly had come back in the middle of summer and had been renovating the bed and breakfast, which was due to reopen in a matter of weeks. Molly was a sweet girl, energetic and friendly and full of life, nothing at all like her old biddy aunt who'd tried to kill the new town librarian. After she'd killed the old one. Naturally Molly knew nothing of her aunt's misdeeds. If she did she'd be shocked. It would break her naive heart.

It was hard to like Molly Duncan. She was everything Ivy Franklin was not.

A couple times a month two or three more people—not a Non-Springer among them—returned. With each new resident, it was as if the magic in the little town grew stronger. It was almost tangible, the sensation of magic, of power old and new. Ivy felt more and more out of sync with every day that passed; with every new resident or business. Once she'd truly belonged here. Now... she wasn't so sure.

Was it too late to get on the bandwagon to cast a spell to isolate this town? That would stop the growth here and now. No one in, no one out...

She was tied to Mystic Springs by magic and by blood. Leaving town would break her. Right out of high school she'd given it a try. She'd moved to Georgia, where she'd attended college for a full year. It had been the worst year of her life, and that was saying something. She'd lost her mother at the age of thirteen, then her father less than ten months later. An aneurysm had claimed her mother. It had happened so fast, too fast. That entire year had been a nightmare. They said her father had a heart attack, but she'd always believed it had

simply been broken by the loss of his wife. She still believed that.

You'd think in a town lousy with magic every resident would be blessed with good health and a long life. Sometimes that was the case, but for the most part Springers were just like ordinary people. They got sick, they had accidents, they suffered from devastating bouts of bad luck. Some had great genetics, others not so much.

She and Eve had never had to worry about a place to live, a roof over their heads and food on the table. An elderly aunt had taken them in and loved them with all her witch's heart. That had been a terrible time, a hellish year, and still, her time away from Mystic Springs had been worse in some ways. Every day, a part of her had faded away. Every day, every hour, she'd felt... less. Smaller, weaker. She'd wasted away. Being apart from Eve had only made things worse. She might as well have cut off a limb and left it behind.

If she left town for good she'd not only lose her magic, she'd lose her twin. She'd lose Eve forever, because if she ever left she wouldn't come back.

So here she stayed, always at loose ends, never satisfied with her life though she did her best to convince herself she was *completely* satisfied, thank you very much. As much as she hated to admit it, she was fading away as surely as she had when she'd left town all those years ago.

The door to her shop opened, and in walked Levi Redmon. Doctor Levi, some of his patients called him. He was in his early thirties, blond-haired and blue-eyed and ridiculously fit. Every morning before his office opened he jogged past her front window, making a loop through town. Show off. Every afternoon, usually after his lunch break, he stopped by her bakery for something sweet. Since her baked goods had no calories, he was in no danger of ruining his hard-won physique.

She wasn't familiar with the Redmon family's history; she

wasn't sure what his magic was, and she didn't ask. Seems like there might've been a healer in his family a few generations ago, but she hadn't seen any extraordinary powers from him as he treated his patients. He was a good doctor, at least he seemed to be, but there was nothing mystical in his methods.

As with many Springer families, the Redmons had mingled magics through marriage over the years. Even that didn't mean anything. Some Springers possessed great magic; others just a touch. Even though Ivy's gifts were a part of her, they only came alive when she was in the kitchen, baking. In spite of the growth of power in the town, she remained the same. A great baker who was able to produce decadent treats that would never cause those who consumed them to gain so much as an ounce. That was it. In the scheme of things, it didn't seem like anything special.

Levi Redmon had already asked her on a date. Four times. She'd rebuffed him firmly each time. Asking for personal details about his family, his past, his magic, if he had any of consequence, might give him the wrong impression. She was *not* interested.

He smiled brilliantly as he ordered two cupcakes and a bear claw and placed the correct change on the counter. Oh, God, he had that look again. A little nervous, a little excited. His nose twitched. He was going to ask her out.

While everyone else in town seemed perfectly happy to pair up and reproduce, Ivy was having none of it. She'd been happy once, thank you very much, and it hadn't ended well. Why tempt fate?

Sure enough, Redmon caught her eye over the counter. "Next weekend..."

Silas burst through the front door, red-faced and sweating even though the early October weather was temperate. Judge, the bloodhound, was at his heels.

"We dragged a man out of the river," Silas said, directing the news to the town's new doctor. "We've moved him to your office.

Susan has a key, and to be honest I didn't know what else to do with the poor guy. He's in pretty bad shape."

Levi followed Silas onto the street, where they both broke into a jog. Judge led the way.

Ivy breathed a sigh of relief as they disappeared from sight. Saved by the bell! Well, saved by the town dog-whisperer. Then she realized Levi had paid but not taken his purchases, which meant he'd be back.

It was hours later when her brother-in-law Travis, the town's one and only lawman, walked into the bakery. He had a look of real concern on his face. That was odd for him. He was an even-tempered guy, hard to rattle, easy to read. It was rare to see him without a happy-go-lucky smile on his face. Eve, Ivy's twin, was part of the reason he smiled so often.

He made his wife happy. She made him happy. Gag.

"Can you come to the doc's office with me? You could close a little early, right?"

She often did. Her bakery was open when she felt like being here, closed when she did not. What now? Ivy knew there wasn't anything wrong with Eve. If there was, she'd know it. She'd feel it.

"Why?" The question was blunt. Unfriendly, maybe, but she never beat around the bush. Some might call her blunt. She preferred the description *direct*.

"I'd like you to have a look at the fella that washed up on the riverbank this morning."

"Again, why?"

Travis was obviously uncomfortable. It was a good thing he'd never be called on to go undercover, because every thought, every emotion, was clearly displayed on his pretty face. "I think I recognize the guy, but he's in bad shape and it's been a long time since I saw him."

"If you can't identify him what makes you think..." She

stopped speaking suddenly, as a chill washed over her. It couldn't be. Impossible. "Grant?"

"I think so," Travis said in a low voice.

Ivy didn't move from her spot behind the counter. "That's not possible. I took him to the edge of town and gave him enough amnesia punch to wipe Mystic Springs from the minds of a dozen men." Not just Mystic Springs, but *her*. That had been the point, right? Allow him to follow his dream. Send the man she loved away so he could have the life he wanted and deserved. He'd worked so hard all his life. She wouldn't...

"It's been more than five years!" She snapped. Five years and four months, to be exact.

"Maybe I'm wrong," Travis said. "Just... have a look."

Still, she didn't make a move. "Why don't you just ask him his name?"

"He doesn't remember anything right now."

"Surely he has some kind of ID on him."

"Nope."

"Ask anyone!" Ivy snapped. "He's a freaking star shortstop, any baseball fan can tell you..."

"His face is bruised and swollen so I can't be sure," Travis argued, "but there's something about him that's familiar. You knew him best. If anyone can identify him, it's you."

"Put out the word!" Ivy argued. "There are a dozen people in town who could identify Grant, if that's who it is." Bruised or not, battered beyond recognition? Her heart skipped a beat. Was it Grant? How badly was he injured? Was he... dead or dying? She didn't want to know, didn't want to see him that way. "Find someone else." *Please.*

"I'm trying to keep this low profile, if I can," Travis said. "The man, whoever he is, he didn't just fall out of a boat or slip and fall off a bridge upriver." He sighed, indicating that this entire situation was a big pain in his ass. "He was shot."

~

Ivy refused to run, but her heart was beating a mile a minute. As she walked quickly down the sidewalk toward the new doctor's office, which was just past the grocery store, she developed tunnel vision. Nothing existed but the path directly ahead. Everything to the side was gray, indistinct. Travis was talking, but she couldn't understand a word he said. It was all gibberish.

Grant Whitlock had stumbled into Mystic Springs on a particularly warm May day more than five years ago. He'd gotten lost and taken a wrong turn. That didn't happen often, and when it did there was usually a reason. Non-Springers didn't end up in Mystic Springs accidentally. If they found their way in, they were meant to be here. After a week, Ivy had convinced herself that Grant's reason for being here was her.

He'd graduated from Vanderbilt, played triple-A ball for a couple of years, and after a minor injury had been summarily cut from the team. The club had recruited a bevy of young talent, new blood, and had let a few of those who'd been around more than a year loose. Grant's injury had been the straw that broke the camel's back, to hear him tell it.

After a lifetime of a focus on baseball, when it was gone he'd felt at loose ends. Rudderless. Not knowing what might come next, he hit the road. A road trip to clear his head, he'd said, to take time to think about what might come next for him. The road had led him to Mystic Springs. To her.

She'd never known anyone like him, had never imagined that any man could make her feel the way he did. Grant had made her laugh. Even as a child, she hadn't been one to laugh often. She wasn't easily entertained. Eve had laughed and smiled enough for both of them.

Grant had sauntered into her bakery looking for something sweet, and instead he'd found her. If there was such a thing as love at first sight, that would be proof. He'd been wandering, but

once he'd found her he'd stayed. They'd been drawn together quickly and completely, and she had to admit, the sex had been stellar. She'd fallen in love. So had he. That love was everything she'd ever dreamed love could be; it was perfection. She'd been deliriously happy, for a while. They'd been together for a little more than a month. If she really wanted to torture herself she could count the days.

A lot had happened during those days...

Then he'd gotten the call. A different AAA team was in need of a shortstop thanks to a few injuries of their own. One of the assistant coaches had been at Vanderbilt and remembered Grant. This coach had been impressed by Grant's abilities, and assured him there was a strong possibility he'd be in the Major Leagues by the following year, maybe even in September if he did the work and luck was on his side. It had to happen fast; Grant was expected to report to his new team in a matter of days.

He'd been over the moon; he'd asked her to go with him.

She'd said no.

It had broken her heart, but after her year in college she'd realized she could never leave Mystic Springs. It was home. It was a part of her body and soul. Without this blessed or cursed place, she had no magic. Maybe she wasn't a powerful witch. She couldn't make it snow like Jordan, or help people realize what they needed like the Benedicts. She didn't change with the moon or like Clint Maxwell shift into a powerful creature whenever the spirit moved him. She didn't control fire or water, or talk to animals, or cast powerful spells.

Still, without her magic, unimpressive as it was, she was nothing.

Grant had told her he didn't need baseball, that he'd turn down the offer and stay with her. There was no guarantee of success in his sport, he knew that. He could wash out in a matter of weeks, months, maybe a year or two. Making it to the Major Leagues was still nothing more than a dream.

Wherever you are, that's where I want to be.

He'd believed those words as he'd spoken them, she'd seen that much. She'd also seen the heartbreak that came with the death of a lifelong dream. Maybe success wasn't guaranteed, but not to even try...

She'd lied to him and told him she'd changed her mind; she'd go with him. Anywhere, any time. All she asked for was a couple of days to get things in order, to say goodbye to her twin.

Was it coincidence that the call had come so soon after they'd done something incredibly impulsive? Only two very young, idealistic people could've been so foolish. She tried not to think about that night, tried not to dwell on what ifs.

He'd agreed to her two days, and they'd spent them well. She'd made love to him at every opportunity; she'd searched her heart for answers she knew she wouldn't find. And when the time came she'd made love to him one last time, driven him to the edge of town, and given him a healthy dose of amnesia punch.

Grant Whitlock had not washed out, after all. He'd gone on to have an impressive career, at least until he'd been injured again last year, late in the season.

As she'd watched him leave, she'd been sure another man would come along, that she'd find what she'd had with Grant with someone else. Next time she'd be sure to fall for a Springer, someone who would truly understand her and why Mystic Springs was so important to her. She'd almost convinced herself that Grant had just been a chapter in her life, not the entire story, and she'd soon be able to move on. But that had never happened. She'd lost a part of herself when she'd sent him away.

Five plus years was a long time. She'd been little more than a child, when she and Grant had been together. Her bakery had been opened less than six months, and she'd made her home on the second floor, in a small apartment. She'd made her life in that building, upstairs at night, downstairs during the day. Grant was a couple of years older than she, but back then had he been more

than a child himself? Not by much. He'd stayed with her in that room above the bakery, for a while. The space had been too small for one, much less for two, but neither of them had cared. Does anyone love as enthusiastically as the young? She thought not.

Redmon's office wasn't often busy. The people of Mystic Springs were healthy, for the most part. There were exceptions, of course. Her parents; Clint's, too. But the elderly needed some extra attention, and there was the occasional broken bone or mysterious rash. And of course, pregnancies. So many pregnancies...

A small waiting room faced the street. The chairs were uncomfortable, and the large front window let in too much afternoon light. At the far end of the room was an unmanned receptionist's desk which held a sign-in sheet and a potted plant that wasn't thriving. Beyond the single door just past that desk, a hallway opened onto four rooms. Three examining rooms and the doctor's office.

The man who'd been shot was in the first room on the right. He reclined on the examining table, eyes closed. His dark brown hair was mussed; his face was indeed bruised and swollen, as Travis had said. A sheet covered the lower half of his body; she could see the thick bandage that had been well-taped to his right side. Maybe that was where he'd been shot.

Ivy wanted to rip the sheet away and examine every inch of his body for more injuries, for more signs of violence. She didn't. Instead she stepped to his side and covered him to the neck with the thin sheet.

"He's cold," she explained, glancing up at Travis.

"Is it Grant?"

Ivy didn't answer, not right away. She looked her fill, noted the changes. He was bigger, more muscular than she remembered. He wore his hair differently, she could tell even though it was wet and messy with a streak of river mud on one side. The changes were no surprise. She was pretty sure he'd cut his own

hair with a pair of clippers back in the day, and these days he could afford the best stylists. There were a few lines on his face that hadn't been there five years ago. She had a few new lines of her own, at the ripe old age of twenty-nine.

"It's him," she whispered, not taking her eyes from the face of the man she'd once loved to distraction.

"Who would've shot him?" Travis mused.

Why did he ask her? She wasn't psychic, and she knew nothing about Grant's personal life these days.

Well, she only knew what she read on the internet. She tried not to obsess, not to look often, but some days she couldn't help herself. Grant Whitlock had been one of the best shortstops in the game, for a while. Watching him was like watching a ballet dancer, tight white pants and all. He made moves no mortal should be able to make. Jumping, twisting, all but flying through the air as he made plays that had the announcers gasping and the fans screaming. All that was before the ACL injury a little more than a year ago. A dirty slide had taken him out as he covered second base. She'd watched the video over and over again, cringing every time she watched his leg buckle unnaturally.

She'd given way too much thought to revenge on the opposing player who'd hurt Grant, but of course she never followed through. That would mean leaving Mystic Springs. Besides, what could she do? Not much.

He'd spent the past year recovering, resting for a while then in intensive rehab. A couple of months ago he'd returned to the field. His moves were not the same; announcers liked to say, again and again, that he'd "lost a step." His team hadn't advanced to the playoffs this season. She'd purposely not done an internet search to find out if Grant would be returning to the sport, or if the dirty slide had cost him his career.

Whenever she surrendered to insomnia and went to the computer with Grant on her mind, she regretted it later. The pictures of him broke her heart. It never got easier. He'd been engaged for a while, but it hadn't worked out. The engagement, with a popular but really annoying TV actress, hadn't lasted a full six months.

The actress was a redhead. Coincidence? Probably. No, definitely. He would have no memory of her *at all*. As she'd intended.

Who would've shot him? That was the kicker here. Grant had been paid well, *very* well, especially in the past three years. Money might've been a motive. Fans could be crazy. She knew damn well that he could drive a woman crazy…

"Someone in town will be able to suss it out," she said too sharply. "Eventually." It would be nice if there was a reliable psychic in town who saw everything they needed and wanted. Life wasn't that simple, not even in Mystic Springs. Not ever, not anywhere. Magic was a part of their lives but it didn't mean they didn't suffer from loss, pain, indecision. No one, psychic or not, could save them from the pain of life.

No psychic was capable of solving all their mysteries.

At the moment the most powerful psychics in town were in the old folks' home and the K-12 school. None of them were entirely reliable.

Grant's eyes fluttered open. With hooded eyes he stared at her. He wouldn't know her, couldn't. Amnesia punch did its job too well. The flicker of recognition she thought she saw in his green eyes was nothing more than a product of her imagination.

Travis seemed to be asking questions. Ivy ignored him. So did Grant.

Then the man she had once loved whispered, "Ivy?"

CHAPTER 2

Red hair, thick and long and luxurious, fell toward him. Blue-green eyes the color of a Caribbean sea captivated him. He said something, but he wasn't sure what or why. The darkness he'd been swimming in claimed him again and he drifted down and down, into a sleep so deep it was like death. Maybe it was death.

His eyes opened again. He had no way of knowing how much time had passed. Might've been minutes, or several hours. Days? No, he didn't think it had been that long. The red-haired woman was still here, looking as if she was both concerned and angry, along with two other men who leaned over him. Frowning. Talking. A doctor and a lawman; he could tell by their clothing. The lawman wore a khaki uniform. The doc wore a traditional white coat.

He hurt all over, but wasn't sure why. He didn't know where he was, and as he searched for some focus, a bit of clarity, he realized he also didn't know *who* he was. His breath caught in his throat; his heart raced. For a moment he felt as if he were drowning; as if all the answers he searched for were above the surface, but the surface was too far away. A name, *his* name, danced just out of reach. He couldn't quite grasp it.

The people taking care of him would know. *She* would know.

The two men were closer than the redhead was, but his eyes stayed on her. Something about her made him feel more in control, not quite so lost. The expression on her face was not at all welcoming, but he felt a strange sort of peace when he looked at her. A calm, even though she appeared anything but calm. He knew her. He had to know her. Why else would he feel this way? The sight of a stranger wouldn't soothe him.

The lawman was talking, asking questions he barely understood. He should concentrate but it was difficult. If only his head would clear; if only he could grasp where and why and who he was.

Finally, a snippet of a question—*shot you*—made its way to his brain, and he turned his gaze up at the lawman.

The man—a small brass name tag read Chief Benedict—asked his question again.

"Who shot you?"

I've been shot? The words were there, but didn't make it out of his mouth. The ache at his side intensified and again, he felt as if he were underwater, sinking fast. He lifted a hand and rested it on a thick bandage, looked to the redhead for a dose of comfort, and finally managed to say the words, garbled as they were. "I was shot?"

He glanced around the room. This looked to be a doctor's office, not a hospital. He wasn't in a bed, he was lying on a padded but hard examining table. There was a calendar on one wall, near a drawing of the heart with its elements marked as if for a classroom. A generic landscape hung on the other wall, just on the other side of the redhead.

The doctor's name was on his chest. No brass nameplate for this one. His name was embroidered, dark blue on the white lab coat. Doctor Redmon.

"Do you know where you are?" Redmon asked.

"No."

"Can you tell me your name?"

He tried again to grasp the name that danced just out of reach. It was frustrating that he couldn't quite manage but the panic was fading. He was no longer drowning. "No."

The two men looked at one another, exchanging a private, silent message of concern.

"We should hand him over to the county sheriff, maybe transport him to the hospital in Eufaula," Redmon said.

"No." The chief's response was immediate and firm.

He was just lucid enough to find that response concerning. Maybe he didn't know who or where he was, but he was clear-headed enough to understand that in normal circumstances a hospital would be a good place for someone who'd been shot.

"Why not?" the doctor asked, clearly frustrated.

Benedict hesitated, looked down at the patient on the table, and frowned. "I don't think it's what he needs. Let me ask around."

As odd as that statement was, neither the doctor nor the redhead seemed concerned by it.

Ivy nudged Travis out of the way. A year ago she would've found his words alarming, since the Benedict family gift of knowing what people needed seemed to have skipped him entirely. Until now. Until everything had started to change. His ability, inconsistent as it was, was coming to life. Slowly, but unmistakably.

"We can't leave Grant here until you decide what to do with him," she said. The examining room was insufficient, the table he was laying on too uncomfortable. "Where is he going to stay?"

She almost offered her house. There was a spare bedroom, after all. But the idea of having the man she'd once loved living under her roof was too much to take.

"Grant?" he said. "Is that my name?"

Ivy sighed. She should've been more careful, but then what difference did it make if he knew his own name?

"Did I have a driver's license?" he asked.

She could hear the confusion in his voice, as well as the desperation to know the truth.

The truth. *I loved you. I married you. I sent you away so your dreams could come true, because that's what you do when you love someone to the depths of your soul.* She couldn't say any of that. No one but the preacher in Eufaula knew about the wedding, and he'd died two years ago. Maybe the preacher's wife would remember, but she was ninety if she was a day and she'd served as witness at a lot of ceremonies.

It didn't matter. The marriage wasn't even legal; they'd not filed any papers at the county courthouse. That didn't mean the words had been any less real. To her, anyway.

"No ID," she said. "You passed through town several years ago. I have a bakery, and you were a regular customer for a while. I remembered your name."

"You must have a great memory."

"I do." And it wasn't always a blessing.

"What town?" he asked.

"Mystic Springs," Travis said, saving Ivy the trouble. "Alabama," he added.

Grant grunted. "Never heard of it. I don't remember…" He smiled, a little. "Okay, I don't remember much of anything at the moment, so I guess that's no surprise." He looked up at Redmon. "When will my memory come back?"

The doctor patted Grant's hand in a way that was probably meant to be comforting. "You've been through a traumatic experience. Give yourself time."

Grant frowned. "I'm not feeling particularly patient at the moment. I need answers. Who would've shot me? Why?"

"That's the million dollar question," Travis grumbled.

"Where is he going to stay?" Ivy asked again. "Someone's

going to have to keep an eye on him, clean his bandage, ar
maybe even protect him if whoever tried to kill him shows up
finish the job. I work, you and Eve work and she's pregnant a
tired all the time. She doesn't need anything else to worry abc
Who's going to have the time to care for him until you dec
what to do?"

Travis smiled, that crooked grin that was so often on his f
That smile was probably one of the reasons Eve had fallen in
with him. Even Ivy found it occasionally charming. "There
couple of vacant rooms at The Egg."

"The egg?" Grant repeated, confused.

"Perfect," Redmon said. "I'm there several afternoons a
anyway, so it won't raise any eyebrows if I'm in and out
than usual. Staff can take care of Grant, when I'm not arour

"The egg?" Grant said again, more insistently this time.

"The Mystic Springs Retirement Home for the Except
Gifted," Ivy said. "Once upon a time it was called the A
Home for the Exceptionally Gifted, but once they put
Mystic Springs Retirement Village sign that changed.
the Exceptionally Gifted part stuck, so it's The Egg for sh

"You're putting me in an old folk's home for wha
artists?" He touched a hand to his stubbled cheek. "Am I?

If only. No, Grant was still young, fit, and handsom
he was an old man, maybe she wouldn't be so tempted
that he come home with her.

A look of concern passed over Grant's battered face
think whoever shot me will be back? I don't want to p
of old people in danger by being there."

"You should be safe," Travis said calmly. "Until we
you were shot, and by whom, there's no need to
shrugged. "Might've been an accident, for all we know

An accident. Ivy wasn't at all psychic, but she didn'

CHAPTER 3

It was well past dark when Chief Benedict transported Grant—he still wasn't entirely sure that was his name but that's what he'd been told and he couldn't argue—to the old folk's home. You'd think by ten at night all the residents would be asleep, but the lobby was brightly lit. Crowded, too, judging by the number of people he saw through the glass double doors. Benedict led him into that lobby, supporting him on one side. As soon as they were indoors a large man scurried from the front desk and added his assistance on the other side. Together they led Grant to a waiting wheelchair, where he gratefully sat. His legs felt like jelly. The wound on his side burned. All he wanted to do was sleep.

Murmuring voices swirled around him.

"Is his hair supposed to look like that?"

"He looks kinda familiar."

"I wonder if he likes brownies?"

"I hear he has amnesia."

"Amnesia? What is this, a soap opera?"

"I haven't made a cabbage casserole in ages. Maybe he'd ke..."

Several voices supplied enthusiastic *nos*.

Grant turned his head toward the crowd. He was so tired, everyone looked blurry, indistinct. Then again, maybe that had something to do with the pain killers the doctor had given him. There were lots of gray heads, a few bald ones, and one that was an unnatural red. That red made him think of the woman who'd been at the doctor's office earlier in the day.

Ivy. That's what the others had called her. Ivy. It was a good name, and it suited her. He'd been hard pressed to keep his eyes off of her, and had missed her when she'd left. How could you miss someone you didn't know? Did she remind him of someone?

The doctor said his memory would return, but he couldn't say when. Maybe in the morning, if he was lucky. Maybe he'd wake up and it would all come rushing back.

He didn't feel like a criminal, he really hoped he wasn't one, but why else would he be in a position to be shot? He'd been going through the possibilities for the past several hours. A hunting accident? An accidental discharge? Did he have enemies? He searched his mind, but with no memories how was he supposed to find answers?

A gray-haired woman who introduced herself as Helen leaned down and in close. Too close. "You'll be right next door to me," she said with a wide smile. If you need anything, anything at all…"

"Leave the man alone, Nana," Benedict said in a soft voice. "You don't need to worry yourself. He won't be here long."

What did that mean? Was he going to have a speedy recovery or did the Chief expect to arrest him, sooner rather than later? If he was a criminal it wouldn't be hard to identify him. Had they taken his fingerprints, at some point? He didn't know, couldn't remember everything that had happened during the day.

Would Benedict put him next door to his grandmother and a bunch of other elderly folks if he thought there would be any danger to them? That wouldn't make sense at all.

Grant's eyes focused on the old woman, Nana, Helen, and he said, "I hate cabbage."

She smiled widely. "See? He's remembering things already."

~

Ivy had spent half the night baking, as she often did when she was out of sorts. She'd been out of sorts a lot lately.

Her bakery did an excellent business, not only because the goodies she baked were divinely delicious, but because they were calorie-free. Some might actually be called healthy. Her twin Eve owned and operated the cafe next door. Eve's food sparked emotion, memories, feelings. And it did have calories. Their gifts had been passed down for generations, though everyone's abilities were a bit different. They fed people; they offered sustenance that was more than what the body required. They fed the soul as well.

Ivy walked into The Egg at 8 a.m. She really shouldn't be here, but after a night of baking there was no way she could sell all these goodies before they went stale. She didn't have the ability to keep old baked goods fresh; that wasn't part of her magic. So she dropped a lavender box of cookies at the front desk, and two boxes of sweet rolls in the downstairs dining room. The fourth box was for Grant. All his favorites. Or what used to be his favorites.

Lemon bars. Strawberry cupcakes. Brownies, some with walnuts and some without.

The Grant she'd known hated walnuts. Would the brownies jog his memory at all?

They'd told Grant his full name, but nothing else. If he knew who he was, he'd find a way to locate someone from his life to collect him. Help him. Get involved in the investigation. That could be a disaster. Not only did Travis believe Grant needed to be here, another Non-Springer coming to town, especially now when things were so lively, wouldn't be the best solution. So they'd keep him close, find out who shot him and make sure he was safe, then when the time was right, see him out of town. Where he belonged.

She really should leave him to Travis and the doc and steer clear, but he'd called her name before anyone else had used it. He shouldn't know her name. He shouldn't remember it or her or Mystic Springs. As his more recent memory came back, would he also remember what he should not?

Amnesia punch was foolproof. Wasn't it? It always had been, where Non-Springers were concerned.

His door was unlocked and she slipped into the apartment quietly. Like the other rooms on this floor, there was a galley kitchen, a sitting room, and one small bedroom. She placed the box of sweets on the kitchen counter and crept silently to the open bedroom door.

Her heart almost stopped when she saw him. If anything the bruises on his face were worse than they'd been yesterday. He slept as he always had, sprawled across the bed on his back, arms flung out, legs spread. A sheet covered him to the waist, so she couldn't be sure that he still slept naked.

She wanted to check. She didn't dare.

His eyes opened slowly and landed on her. "You," he whispered. He didn't seem at all surprised to see her.

Her heart did a wild dance. Her heart, or her stomach, or both. "Ivy," she said. "My name's Ivy."

"I know." He tried to sit up, then thought better of it. "I heard Benedict say your name yesterday." That statement was followed by a frown. "You two seemed close, is he your..."

"Brother-in-law," she said when he faltered.

"Good," he whispered.

Why good? What difference could it possibly make to him if she was married or had a boyfriend? She didn't dare to ask.

"I brought you some sweets from my bakery. I didn't know

what you'd like, so there are a few different things in the box. I left it on the kitchen counter."

He lifted a hand. "Help me up."

"No!" She didn't want to touch him, couldn't. Wouldn't.

"I need to go to the bathroom, and I don't think I can get out of this bed on my own."

She could call someone on the staff to help him, but it's not like he was asking her to change his bandage. It would be weird for her to refuse. He might wonder why she was so damned and determined not to touch him.

"Fine." She stepped to the side of the bed and took his hand. It felt just as it had five years ago; it felt the way it did in her dreams. Large and strong and calloused. One touch, and she was lost.

They'd always had chemistry.

He stood and steadied himself. For a moment, Ivy was relieved. He was not sleeping naked, but wore a pair of silky blue boxers. Were they his or a loaner? There had been time for someone to launder his clothes, but had they? It didn't matter. She was just glad he wore those boxers. She wasn't ready to face a naked Grant.

Her gaze flittered down to his left knee. It was scarred; he'd had at least two surgeries there. Looking at those scars her anger grew, and she wondered if she could work up the courage to leave Mystic Springs and get the revenge she'd dreamed of in the past. Though last time she'd checked the dirty ballplayer was in California. It would be a long way to go for a little payback in the name of a man who wouldn't ever remember her. Besides, any magic she possessed would be gone by the time she travelled that distance.

She reminded herself that some poisons didn't require any magic at all, but she quickly rejected the notion. Well, she rejected it, maybe not as quickly as she should've.

Grant seemed stronger than he had yesterday. Hand to hand

was all that would be required. And dammit, that was enough. Just his hand in hers made her heart pound. He stood there a moment, found his balance, then took a step and stumbled into her. She caught and steadied him.

"Sorry," he said with a crooked smile. "I guess it's a good thing you stopped by."

Her heart was pounding and her knees were weak, and he seemed to be entirely unaffected.

Okay, maybe not entirely unaffected.

His head turned slightly. "You smell really good."

"Side-effect of owning my own bakery."

"No, it's not that. You're..." He looked into her eyes. He really shouldn't do that.

"Let's go." She steered him toward the small bathroom. It was designed for an elderly resident, so there were handrails everywhere. At the door, she watched as he grabbed onto one and then she released him. "You're on your own."

She closed the door and leaned against the wall. If she was smart she'd bolt now. He could find his way back to bed on his own, right? She could send up a staff member to take care of him, and if he fell before that happened, well, it wouldn't be the worst injury he'd suffered in the past couple of days.

But she stayed, listened to him pee and flush and run water in the sink. As soon as he opened the bathroom door, she offered her support. Again, what choice did she have?

"Why don't you like me?" he asked as they took slow, deliberate steps back toward the bed.

"What makes you think I don't like you?" she snapped.

"Your face," he said, and then he smiled, a little.

"It's just my face, dumbass."

Instead of being insulted, he laughed.

"It's called resting bitch face," she said. "Don't take it personally."

Being this close to Grant was blissful and torturous, at the same time. She loved touching him, taking in his body heat, feeling his weight as he leaned gently into her. The feelings were wonderful, but also so damned painful.

He sat on the side of the bed then slipped under the covers, sighing as he got comfortable. Well, as comfortable as possible in his current state. He sighed once, then said, "I'd really like to see you smile."

"Don't hold your breath."

CHAPTER 4

Breakfast was delivered by a man in blue nurses' scrubs. Eggs, bacon, biscuits, grits. Grant ate every bite, drank a glass of orange juice and two cups of coffee. Ivy had bolted too fast, once breakfast had arrived. She'd told him about the baked goods she'd left in the kitchen, but he didn't have the strength to walk into that room and check them out. Later, if he had a burst of energy.

Would she come back? Maybe. Then again, maybe not. She wasn't exactly what he'd call the Welcome Wagon type. At least, that wasn't the face she presented to the world. There was more to her, he was sure of it.

Other people were in and out of his room during the day. It was hard to get more than a half hour of sleep without interruption. The doctor checked on him and changed his bandage, reassuring him that while it was nasty enough, it could've been worse. The doc gave a cursory glance to the scars on the side of his left knee. Whatever had happened there had healed well, but wasn't exactly pretty. Looked like surgery scars, not a wound inflicted by violence.

Those scars were not new, but he'd very recently been shot.

That should be what was on his mind more than some unfriendly redhead, but it wasn't.

The woman he'd met in the lobby last night, Helen, stopped by with a couple of her friends. Ginger and Ramona. The two elderly friends checked him out as if he'd sprung a second head or an eye in the middle of his forehead, while his neighbor acted as if having a man who'd been shot in the room next to hers was a normal thing. They left yet more food in the kitchen. Cookies and a casserole, one of them said. He hoped it wasn't cabbage.

Chief Benedict came by that afternoon. He asked a few questions, none of which Grant could answer. Grant asked a couple of questions of his own. *Why do I need to be here? What the hell does that even mean?* Benedict just shrugged and said he'd stop by tomorrow. He didn't seem concerned by the memory loss, or anything else. No handcuffs appeared, so maybe Grant Whitlock, whoever he was, wasn't a wanted man, after all.

When the last of his visitors left, Grant fell into a deep sleep. He dreamed of cupcakes and a sexy redheaded baker.

Ivy closed for the day and started walking. No matter the season, no matter the time of day, she walked to and from work daily. She had warm jackets, raincoats and umbrellas, boots suitable for rain or winter or both. Not that they got severe winter weather here in South Alabama very often, but what little cold they experienced was usually damp and more than cold enough for her.

The days were getting shorter, but there was still some light in the sky. The cafe was hopping, and would stay busy until closing time. Ivy spotted her twin through the window. A quick search showed that Travis was sitting at the counter, as he did most nights.

Ruby, who was currently waiting on a couple at one of the booths, had turned out to be a really great employee. She'd recently rented James Garvin's old house on Magnolia Road and said she was saving so one day she could buy it. A lot of work would be necessary to bring the neglected place back to life, but if anyone could do that, it was Ruby. She was more than happy to work extra hours, the customers loved her, and with her short dark hair, deep brown eyes, and easy smile, she brought the single men into Eve's Cafe in droves.

What would Eve do as her pregnancy progressed? What would she do after the baby was born? Eve had a couple of more than competent employees in addition to Ruby who could make coffee and tea and wait on customers, but she did all the cooking. Would that change? Hell, everything else had, why not that? Ruby was capable, and she had the right kind of personality for running the place, if it was necessary.

But if Eve didn't cook the food, it wouldn't be special. It would just be... food.

It blew Ivy's mind more than a little that her twin was pregnant. God, more Benedicts. Just what this town didn't need. Mike's wife Cindy was due any day, and Jordan Benedict, Luke's wife, was just into her second trimester. They'd wasted no time at all starting a family, after their summer wedding.

When Ivy got to her street, she didn't turn. She'd intended to, she really had, but her legs carried her forward. Past the grocery store, past the shuttered doctor's office, on toward The Egg.

At the end of downtown proper, something caught her eye and she turned her head. Someone had been painting on the concrete block side wall of what was now a chocolate shop. Graffiti in Mystic Springs. She'd never thought to see the day. She stopped for a moment and checked out the art. It was art, she had to admit, more like the beginning of a mural than out and out defacement. High on the wall there were stars painted on a night sky. Those stars shimmered as if they were almost alive. Still...

"Vandals," Ivy whispered before she left the graffiti behind and resumed her walk.

It was foolish of her to even consider checking on Grant again. Whatever they'd had, once upon a time, was over. It had ended years ago. She might sometimes lie awake at night wondering if she'd made the right decision for him and for herself, but he hadn't suffered a single sleepless night over her. She'd made sure of that, hadn't she? She didn't know why he'd called her name when he'd first opened his eyes; it shouldn't have happened.

The marriage—which didn't really count, she reminded herself—had been an impulse. The night had been beautiful and warm. They'd fallen in love so hard it seemed there was no one else in the world but the two of them. Neither of them wanted to get engaged, they didn't want to call family and friends and spend months planning a ceremony, but they didn't want to wait a minute longer to be man and wife. So they'd hopped in Grant's car, driven to Eufaula, and rounded up a preacher who'd been initially reluctant. Grant had won the old man and his wife over, and the ceremony had taken place then and there.

Ivy had reasoned they could get married again, with people in attendance, if they wanted or needed to. For three lovely, blessed, wonderful days, they'd been secretly man and wife. She'd loved their secret, had reveled in it.

And then he'd gotten the call.

In spite of the depth of her love, Ivy had been so sure she'd be able to forget Grant. She hadn't. A young and hopelessly naive girl had been certain love would come again. It hadn't.

The truth hurt. Love hadn't come again because she'd shut down that part of herself. She'd regretted her decision as soon as she'd given Grant the amnesia punch. She'd cried for days; she'd gone to the river and screamed at the moon every night for a week straight.

And then she'd grown tired of the pain and she'd shut it all down. The love, the ache, the regrets. Hope.

Seeing him had brought it all back; all but the hope. Dammit, she hurt as much as she had when he'd left.

Maybe he'd be sleeping. She'd look in on him and walk away. She did wonder if he'd eaten any of the baked goods she'd dropped off that morning. Yes, she'd look in, check the lavender box to see what was missing, and then she'd head home to get a good night's sleep to make up for last night's restlessness.

The residents were all at dinner, she supposed. No one was in the lobby. She didn't have to endure chitchat in the elevator. The hallway was clear, as she headed for Grant's room. Just as well. She'd never been what anyone would call super social. Eve was an extrovert, but Ivy was a true introvert and always had been. She didn't want or need people. She'd make a great hermit.

The door to Grant's room was unlocked. She slipped inside, trying to make as little noise as possible. She stepped to the edge of the small kitchen area and lifted the lid of the lavender box. All the lemon bars and one strawberry cupcake had been eaten. One brownie had a single bite taken out of it. It was one of the brownies with walnuts, she noticed.

He hadn't changed.

She had.

From the bedroom, Grant called out a soft, "Hello? Is someone there?"

Ivy sighed. She could ignore the call and slip back into the hallway. He'd never know she'd been here. It's not like he could chase her down in his condition!

But she sighed and headed toward the bedroom. "It's just me," she said. "I thought I'd check in on you, but I'm not sure why."

She stood in the doorway and looked at him. He smiled at her, and holy hell, that smile was as magical as any special abilities she possessed. How else could it reach inside her and grab that way?

"You knew I was thinking about you," he said. "That's why."

She snorted. "As if."

"I *was* thinking about you. The food here has been ok, but

what you brought by this morning, that was special. I was thinking about a strawberry cupcake for dessert."

"So you weren't thinking about me, you were thinking about food. Cupcakes, to be precise."

Again, that grin. "Cupcakes and the woman who delivered them."

Second thoughts washed over her. She shouldn't be here. Grant shouldn't think about her at all. Even when his memories returned, as Redmon said they would, she wouldn't be a part of them. At least, she shouldn't be. She kept remembering how he'd whispered her name when he'd first awakened. She wanted to convince herself that she'd imagined it, but she hadn't. In that moment, at that time, he'd remembered her.

When he left here would she have to give him another batch of amnesia punch? Would that damage him in any way? No one had ever, to her knowledge, been given more than one dose.

This was torture.

She should've gone straight home after work. This was it, her last visit to the man she loved. She wouldn't come back to see him again. What was the point? Travis would investigate and hopefully find out who'd shot Grant. Redmon would patch him up and send him to a hospital or a rehab clinic for recovery.

And she'd be stuck with a newly re-broken heart, with no one to blame but herself.

"I gotta go," she said, her voice too quick and light. With that she turned and all but ran to the door. As she stepped into the hallway, hoping to find herself alone once again, Helen's door opened and a crowd stepped out. Helen, her friends, and—surprise—Felicity Adams and Bria Paine. They must've been visiting their great-grandmothers, Ramona and Ginger.

There was so much magic in that cluster of females, Ivy could almost see it. The women, and the girls, shimmered. The air around them sparkled with life, with power.

"There you are," Ginger said. With that statement she glared at her great-granddaughter. "There's no time like the present. Fess up, girls."

Felicity and Bria were ushered to the front of the crowd. They both looked at the carpet and shuffled their feet, obviously wishing they could slink to the back of the crowd. They could not.

"We meant well, really we did," Felicity said. She glanced up at Ramona. "She's always so sad and angry. Really, *really* angry. We only wished that she could be happy like her sister. It was a nice wish, what's so wrong with..."

"It wasn't a wish," Ramona said sharply. "It was a *spell.* You two should know better. Your power is strong, and volatile, and still growing."

"We didn't know it was a spell, exactly," Bria whispered.

"The heartfelt wish of two developing witches who possess more magic than they realize, cast into the universe on the night of the autumnal equinox," Helen said almost, but not quite, harshly.

"That was two weeks ago!" Felicity said. "We thought maybe it didn't work."

It was Helen who said, through pursed lips, "If you didn't know it was a spell why did the thought that it didn't work even cross your mind?"

Both girls looked at the carpet again. The three older ladies started talking at once.

Ivy lifted a hand to silence them, and wonder of wonders, it worked.

"You cast a spell for my happiness?"

Felicity whispered yes. Bria just nodded her head. Neither of them looked at her. They were both thirteen years old, both pretty and bright and, as Helen had said, more powerful than they knew.

"On the night of the equinox."

Again, nodding heads.

Two days after the equinox, Grant had left the team he'd been with for the past three years, his future uncertain. He was up for contract renewal, but hadn't been signed. Maybe another team would want him, but even though his injury was healing he wasn't the player he'd once been. He'd lost a step, as the sportscasters liked to say, and there was no guarantee that he'd get it back. She'd read all of that online, when she should've been sleeping.

In just under two weeks he'd been set adrift from a career he loved, been shot by persons unknown, and had somehow found his way to the bank of the river just beyond Mystic Springs. He hadn't died, he'd been miraculously found and saved.

He'd remembered her, for a moment.

Was Grant the only way for her to find happiness? She'd been deliriously happy with him, for a while. Could she get that back, even if just for a short time?

What about *his* happiness? Could a wish from these two alone be enough to ensure that he had everything he wanted and needed? Maybe his injury could heal completely—gunshot wound *and* knee—and he could go back to baseball. He could be the comeback story of the decade.

And she'd watch from a distance, as she had for the past five years.

Before that happened, maybe she could be happy again. She'd given up on happiness. It was a childish concept, a vague and fleeting emotion that was as slippery as the mud on the bottom of the river. Who needed it? A taste of real joy just set a person up for a fall when it was taken away. Why take that risk? She'd been content to be crabby Ivy, who hated Non-Springers and change of any kind, and lost herself in baking so she never had to think about what she'd given up. Love. Hope.

Happiness.

It wouldn't last, but maybe...

She reached out and put a finger from each hand under two

young, trembling chins. It didn't take a lot of effort to make the girls look at her.

"What you possess is special. Don't waste it wishing for someone else's happiness." She wasn't the town wise woman, not by a long shot, but she felt compelled to add, "Happiness is always in our own hands. Sometimes we have to work for it. No one else can... no one can make you happy. You have to make it for yourself."

With that she turned around and walked back into Grant's room.

CHAPTER 5

Grant woke from a deep sleep to find Ivy, beautiful Ivy, sitting in a chair by his bed. He liked looking at her. Something about her face soothed him, even when she looked angry. No, angry wasn't quite right. She always looked frustrated.

He was pretty damned frustrated himself but one look at her face and he felt calmed. Anchored. His life was a mess at the moment, but it felt like much less of a mess when she was near. Yes, he did enjoy looking at her, but what he really wanted was to touch her.

He had no idea how long she'd been there, sitting in that hard, uncomfortable chair that had been moved to this room from the small dining table in the main room. Since Ivy always looked, well, the way she looked, he couldn't judge by the expression on her face.

It was fully dark beyond the window, so apparently he'd slept for a while.

"I thought you were going to leave," he said.

"So did I," she said, her voice not quite as terse as it had been at times.

"Did you forget something?" Why else would she come back? Then again, what could she possibly have forgotten?

"No. Yes. I'm not sure."

"You should've woken me up." Grant scooted back and up in the bed. Ivy rose, obviously with the intention of helping him or stopping him, but he held up a hand to still her. He had to be able to maneuver on his own, and the only way to find his limits was to move, to *try*. He was slow, sure enough, but within a couple of minutes he was sitting up with his back to the headboard.

"You really should wear a shirt or a pajama top to bed," Ivy insisted. She pursed her lips in what appeared to be disapproval, but she didn't look away.

"I should not. It's a hundred degrees in here." An exaggeration, but not much of one.

Ivy sighed and then smiled. The smile didn't last long, but he liked it.

"This is an old folks' home, and old folks stay cold," she said. "The temps are set to keep them comfortable."

That could be true, but it didn't make him feel any cooler. "How long am I going to have to stay here?"

Ivy shrugged her shoulders. "Until the doc releases you or Travis arrests you."

He kept hoping a memory or two would come back. Every time he woke, he expected some new tidbit to come to him. So far, nada. There was no evident head injury to account for his amnesia, and he was able to function without issues. He remembered how to brush his teeth, how to speak, and he could remember unimportant things, like favorite books and movies. But when it came to his personal history, there was nothing.

"Why are you here?" he asked.

Ivy seemed to be considering her answer carefully. Then she stood, moved to the bed, and sat. "Do you believe in fairy tales?" she asked.

"I don't know. Do I?"

"Remember Sleeping Beauty? Snow White?"

He did, vaguely. A prince. A sleeping princess. A kiss to awaken. "Are you the prince in this scenario or am I?"

Ivy didn't answer, but leaned in to place her mouth on his. Her touch wasn't overtly passionate; it might be classified as a friendly kiss that lingered a bit too long. And then it changed…

Grant closed his eyes and let the sensations wash over him. For such a simple kiss, it was powerful. This was connection, on a level he couldn't quite grasp in the same way he couldn't grasp his own name. It was a kiss and more than a kiss. An awakening, in the way of the fairy tales Ivy spoke of.

He did not reach out and grab her, though he was tempted. She didn't put her arms around him. There was simply mouth to mouth, her lips on his.

His insides churned; he smelled cinnamon and baking bread, cookies, fresh washed sheets.

And tears.

She pulled away. He almost expected to see the tears he'd smelled, but her eyes and her face were dry.

"Why did you do that?" he whispered.

"Complaining?"

"No."

"Remember anything?"

"No." He reached for her. "But maybe we could try again."

They did. The second kiss was deeper than the first, more passionate, more… more everything. Ivy couldn't be a stranger to him. It was impossible to have this kind of immediate reaction to the touch of a stranger.

They'd kissed before, he knew it. How was that possible? If she knew him as more than a customer, more than a stranger passing through town, why hadn't she told him?

The kiss ended, and Ivy drew away. Already he missed her; he thought about grabbing her and pulling her back, but he didn't. Judging by what little he knew of her, now she'd bolt without a word, leaving him more confused and entranced. But she didn't leave. She sighed, kicked off her shoes, and slipped under the covers.

"I really shouldn't be here," she said as she settled in.

"You'll get no complaints from me."

He was in no shape to take this any further than a kiss and a cuddle, but damned if he didn't want to give it a try.

"Don't try any funny business," she said without heat. "I didn't sleep last night." She yawned and snuggled closer. "I don't want to go home. I want to sleep right here. Do you mind?"

Before he could answer, she was asleep. Just as well. No matter what kind of shape he was in, there was no way he'd ever kick this woman out of his bed. He held her close and eventually slept himself.

Ivy woke to sunlight coming through the window. Her face was pressed into Grant's side, her leg was tossed over his. They were tangled, in the sheets and in each other. This is how it was supposed to be, right? They belonged together. Just lying together was bliss. She was happy.

Grant was the only man who'd ever made her feel this way.

Climbing into his bed had been foolish and impulsive, not at all like her. Though goodness knows she'd been impulsive where Grant was concerned more than once in the past. He called to her. She was drawn to him. He was... irresistible. Ivy Franklin was a woman who prided herself on being able to resist any temptation; Grant was her weakness.

She'd had perfectly good reasons for sending him away, five years ago. And yet... how often had she regretted that choice? Every day, for a long while. Then maybe just once a week or so. She knew now that he'd been the best thing that ever happened to her. Could she reclaim him for a while? She breathed deep, inhaled the scent of the man she loved and treasured it. Why not? Why shouldn't she take whatever happiness life had to offer?

No matter how much she wanted him, it had been foolish to sleep here in Grant's arms. He had no memory of her. She'd done everything possible to drive him out of hers.

She rolled over and found herself face to face with a very unhappy Doctor Redmon. He'd pulled the chair she'd sat in last night closer to the bed, and leaned in to glare at her.

"What the hell are you doing here?" he whispered.

"I was tired," she said, reaching up to straighten her hair. "I came by to check on your patient and pretty much just... passed out." That was close enough to the truth. She didn't want to tell Redmon about Felicity and Bria's spell, about her intention to grab a bit of happiness while she could. She certainly didn't want to tell him that she loved Grant, again, still, always.

"Is he the reason you would never go out with me?" The question was whispered lowly, but Ivy glanced to Grant to make sure he was still deep asleep. He was.

"My reason for not dating you is none of your business."

"Isn't it?"

Something odd flashed in Levi Redmon's eyes. He'd always been so pleasant, so easy-going, such a good guy. He didn't look like a good guy now. Was that jealousy? Envy? There was more than a hint of anger in his eyes.

In an instant, his expression changed. Shifted. His eyes softened; he almost smiled. "I don't want to see you hurt, Ivy. You're always so cautious, not just with me but in your life. Why throw all that aside for a man you once knew? A man who left you?"

I sent him away. She didn't say that out loud. *I still love him.* She didn't say that, either. "Don't worry about me," she said calmly. "I know how to take care of myself."

"Do you? Do you really?"

She didn't answer that time, but slipped cautiously out of the bed, grabbed her shoes, and ran.

~

The bakery opened later than usual, but that didn't matter. Ivy's hours were always whatever suited her on that particular day. If she didn't love her job, she might only open a couple days a week. But she loved baking, and she loved the customers who appreciated what she could do. She didn't really like people all that much, but there was nothing like watching a child take their first bite of an Ivy cupcake, or studying the blissful expression of a customer who walked into the bakery with a smile on their face as they tried to choose from the massive selection under the glass.

Felicity and Bria had been wrong. She *did* have moments of happiness. She was satisfied with her life, most days.

She just didn't have love anymore. And dammit, last night's moment of weakness aside, she didn't *need* love.

Her friend Marnie came bopping in not long after the doors opened. They should not be close. They definitely shouldn't be good friends. Not only was Marnie everything Ivy was not—an optimistic, bubbly chatterbox who saw the best in everyone—she'd been the start of the shift in Mystic Springs. She'd come to town as the new Non-Springer librarian, fallen in love with the town Bigfoot shifter, married him, and had his baby. All in just over a year. All the big changes that had befallen the town had begun with her. Coincidence? Maybe. Maybe not.

Marnie was that odd combination of super annoying and hard not to like.

"Oh my God," Marnie said as she approached the counter. "Tell me what I'm hearing is true."

"What did you hear, and from whom?" Had Levi been gossiping about where and how he'd found her that morning?

"I heard some guy you used to be involved with turned up shot, with amnesia, which I thought was just a thing in, like, books and movies. And I heard he's kinda famous. If he has amnesia does he know he's famous? I guess that doesn't matter, he's famous whether he remembers it or not."

"Who told you all this?"

"Who didn't tell?" Marnie said. "Everyone is talking about it. Sorry, I know you have to hate that, since you're such a private person. I expected a phone call from you, but when that didn't happen I decided to come by and find out for myself."

"Where's the baby?" The newest Maxwell was six weeks old, adorable and cuddly in the way babies are, and the light of Marnie's life. She had about three hundred pictures of the kid on her phone.

"Clint's babysitting. I can't be gone long because Aiden is all about Mama." She hefted her larger than normal boobs. "I'm glad I'm breast-feeding, I really am, but I've had no wine for six months, and I can't go far for very long. The kid has an appetite! So spill and don't dawdle. I want to know everything."

Ivy made coffee—decaf for Marnie, still—and they sat at a table in the far corner. She couldn't eat, couldn't take a bite since her stomach was in knots, but Marnie had a chocolate cupcake and a lemon bar, and seemed to enjoy them both.

She hadn't actually talked about Grant for years. Hadn't wanted to. Sure, several people knew that he'd stayed in town a while, that she'd been crazy about him, that he'd left. Some of them knew that she hadn't been the same since. Maybe they'd drawn their own conclusions, but if they gossiped about her and her broken heart, they did it when she wasn't around.

Which was wise.

Much had changed since Grant's return, so she talked. She told Marnie everything. Well, everything but the marriage bit. Not even Eve knew about that, and since it wasn't legal, what did it matter? Marnie was fascinated. She smiled, she teared up, she got angry in all the right places. She reacted as a true friend would.

She cared.

When Ivy finished Marnie leaned forward and whispered, as if they weren't alone, "What are you going to do?"

Ivy handed Marnie a napkin. "I can't take you seriously when you have chocolate icing on your face." She indicated with one finger where the chocolate had landed, and Marnie wiped her face vigorously.

"There," Marnie said. "Now what?"

"I haven't decided," Ivy said truthfully. She wasn't normally so indecisive, but she'd been going back and forth all morning. Should she take what she wanted, knowing it wouldn't last, or steer clear and harden her heart all over again?

Again Marnie whispered. "I think you should sleep with him. After he's healed, of course."

"Sex is your answer to all my problems," Ivy deadpanned.

"Well, it won't hurt," Marnie argued. "Sex is important! Clint is so..."

"I don't want to hear this," Ivy interrupted.

"I know he's your cousin and all, but really..."

"I'm going to put calories in your cupcakes from here on out if you don't stop talking right now."

Marnie leaned back in her chair, pouted a little, then sighed in resignation. "Fine. Now I know you're serious. When am I going to get to meet this Grant?"

"Never!"

Marnie laughed.

Ivy did not.

Grant looked for Ivy to stop by in the evening again. He waited, like a kid with a schoolboy crush. She didn't show, not that night or the next morning. If he was able he'd walk out of this place and hunt her down. But he wasn't able. Not yet.

The doctor checked his bandage and declared him on the

mend. Chief Benedict dropped by in the afternoon to ask if he remembered anything yet. He did not. Food was delivered three times a day. Helen Benedict, his next-door neighbor for the duration, checked on him half a dozen times. He liked the old lady, even if she was a little bossy. She had a light about her, a life and a liveliness. Throughout the day she kept telling him what he needed, which was weird and yeah, bossy. Three other older women stopped by to drop off food. Brownies. Cookies. Some kind of casserole but again, not cabbage, so maybe Helen had gotten the word out that he wasn't a fan.

And still, no Ivy.

How was it possible to miss someone you barely knew? As if he could say he "knew" anyone. To crave a rare smile, the touch of a hand, the feel of her body lying beside his. Maybe his lack of connection to anyone or anything was why he clung to Ivy, against all reason. Her face had been the first thing he'd seen when he came to in the doctor's office. Was that enough to make him need her this way?

She'd slept with him last night. In the literal sense, at least. She'd curled up against his good side, found her place, and slept hard. At least three times in the night he'd awakened with the oddest sense of comfort, of being certain that she'd been there before, that she belonged at his side.

What he remembered even more vividly were those kisses. Two of them, each one spectacular. It felt right to kiss her. He wanted another kiss more than anything else. More than his memories, more than a quick healing.

At the same time, something nagged at him. Though he couldn't remember anything at all, he felt sure there was someone special in his life. He didn't wear a ring, didn't even remember his own name much less the name of a wife or a fiancée, but an image teased him. A woman in a yellow sundress carrying a bouquet of wildflowers, walking through an empty church toward him. With that image came a feeling of commitment, of dedication, of love. He didn't see a face, just that yellow sundress and the flowers. He couldn't pull up a name, but he was almost certain he had a wife, somewhere.

Would that wife miss him? Report him missing? If she did Chief Benedict would get some kind of notification, he imagined. If that happened, he'd have a name for the woman he was connected to, a confirmation of his own name, and some answers. This was assuming the woman he was beginning to remember wasn't the one who'd shot him…

Close to midnight he walked into the kitchen, wearing nothing but his boxers. He was already moving better than he had since he'd arrived in Mystic Springs, though he wasn't going to win any races or get very far on his own. This room was too damn hot, and though he'd looked around more than once he hadn't found a thermostat he could adjust. He imagined every room in the building was overly warm. He'd opened a couple of windows, which helped. It was a nicely cool October night, and there was a breeze to cut the heat.

The doc was right; his side was healing. The pain there was much less intense than it had been, though he expected it would bother him for a while. As he approached the kitchen counter and the goodies there he looked down and noticed again the scars on the side of his left leg, there at the knee. He'd been so focused on his memory and the gunshot wound, at first he hadn't given much thought to that scar. Today he'd had more than enough time to think. To obsess. The scar was massive, and he'd guess not all that old. Months, maybe, not years. Could that be another clue that might help identify him?

He had several midnight snack options, but he headed straight for the light purple box. There wasn't much left in there, just a couple of brownies with walnuts. He didn't like the nuts, and did his best to pick them out. He never got them all.

But Ivy had made them, and they were damn good. Even with the walnuts.

Why could he remember that he disliked walnuts and cabbage, but his name and everything about his past was gone? He had to take Benedict's word that his name was Grant Whitlock. It didn't strike him as being wrong, but neither did that name spark even a single memory or hint of recognition.

Redmon said his memory would come back eventually, either gradually or all at once. The doc couldn't be sure when or how it would happen, though he seemed certain that it would. It had been a couple of days and dammit, he should be remembering something by now.

Something other than a happy, faceless bride in a yellow sundress...

CHAPTER 6

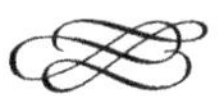

Ivy stayed away from The Egg for three days. For the entirety of those days, she mentally wrestled with herself. As soon as Grant was healed enough he could be sent on his way. Maybe away from Mystic Springs his memory would return. Was his amnesia due to being shot or was it a result of returning to the place where he'd been given amnesia punch? She might never know.

She could ask around; Helen and her bunch might be able to answer questions. Unfortunately, asking those questions would just spur Helen and all to ask their own, and Ivy wasn't ready for that.

Once he was gone things could get back to normal, at least in her life. Grant's? Someone might try to kill him again. His knee might heal enough that he could return to baseball. It was really too soon to know for sure that he was done, baseball-wise. It was very possible that a team would take a chance on him, sign him on and give him the right treatment and more time for a full recovery. It did happen; it could happen for him.

There were those who thought she should grab whatever happiness she could while he was around, and she'd certainly considered doing just that. But wouldn't that be self-inflicted torture? He couldn't stay. All she would do was fall back into love with him and then have her heart broken all over again. Sleep with him, Marnie said. Be happy, Helen Benedict and her gang of witches—young and old—said. Ivy still wasn't sure she was meant to be happy, not ever again.

What would Eve say? Ivy had no idea. She'd avoided her twin all week, because Eve was the only person she could never lie to. The one person who would see right through her, no matter how hard she tried to hide this anguish. If not for Travis and the pregnancy keeping Eve occupied, she would've already been nagging her twin for avoiding her. For once, Ivy was grateful for the distraction that was Travis Benedict.

It was a busy Saturday morning, and she was glad of it. Staying busy might keep her mind off Grant for a few minutes. Marnie was in and out, with baby in arms and a questioning smile Ivy ignored. Several other regulars stopped by, picking their favorites from the case and talking about weekend plans. Magic aside, many of the Springers had real jobs. They enjoyed a couple days off as much as anyone in the world.

Close to noon, Molly Duncan stopped by. As usual, she was annoyingly perky. She picked out a variety of sweet rolls and bar cookies, chattering away as she mused over what else she might add to her order. Why weren't she and Marnie the best of friends? They shared some character traits, that was for sure. So why was Ivy able to get past Marnie's character flaws—like being overly friendly—while Molly put her teeth on edge?

During a pause, Molly peered over the counter and smiled even wider than usual. "You know the guy that got shot?"

Ivy's heart skipped a beat. "Yeah."

"He's improved a lot, and I don't think he's loving staying at The Egg, so Travis asked if he could stay at the B&B for a while. I'm not entirely finished with the renovations, but a few rooms are ready for boarders." She leaned closer. "He's a baseball player. Pretty famous, if you like the sport. Which I don't, but it's still kind of exciting. For some reason we're not supposed to tell him anything about himself, other than his name. I have no idea why, but when it comes to town business I just do what I'm told."

"Why your place?" Ivy asked, her voice deceptively calm. "Why not Eufaula?" Or Montgomery or Birmingham. Anywhere but *here.*

"I think Travis would really like to find out who shot the guy before he lets him loose. He says Grant needs to be here, but he isn't sure why." With that, Molly shrugged. "Works for me. He's really cute! Quite the stud, if you ask me."

Did Molly have romantic plans for Grant? Maybe. There was something different about the gleam in her eye. Cute? Stud? She was obviously interested. Was Ivy willing to step aside and let the bubbly innkeeper have him?

After days of agonizing back and forth, Ivy finally made up her mind. No. No she was not. She was not going to stand back and let some other woman have her man. The possessive thought surprised her a little, but she didn't back away from it.

"Be sure to get some of these apple walnut muffins," Ivy said with a tight smile. "They'll be great for breakfast. And brownies." She gestured to the ones that were heavy with nuts.

Molly ordered several of both.

After the B&B owner was gone, purchases wrapped and stored in a big lavender box she carried carefully, Ivy removed her apron and turned off the purple neon Open sign. She was never indecisive. Okay, *rarely* indecisive. This week's fickleness was an aberration brought on by emotional turmoil. That was the only explanation. Normally once she made up her mind, nothing could stop her.

Ivy headed for the door, then did an about-face and went to the counter. She loaded up a box with cookies of all kinds, and then set out to do what needed to be done. On the sidewalk, with the door to Ivy's Bakery locked behind her, she turned right.

Away from Eve's Cafe, away from home, away from downtown proper.

She didn't walk far. Benedict's Hardware was directly next door.

Lucky for her, Luke was at the counter and seemed to be alone. She gave the big store a quick once over, to be sure no one else was lurking about, then walked to the counter and placed the lavender box in front of him.

"These are for you," she said tersely.

He looked appropriately suspicious. "What's the catch?"

"Be sure to save some of the lemon ice box cookies for Jordan. They're her favorite."

"Thanks. Again, what's the catch? In all the years we've been side by side, you've never brought me cookies. Except for that one time you wanted me to close up the store so I could fix your sink."

Which he'd done without complaint. Well, without *much* complaint.

Ivy sighed. She hated asking for help. Hated it! It went against every instinct she possessed.

"I'd like for you to..." She stopped, stammered, drew a deep breath. "Dammit, Luke, what do I need?"

Grant moved slowly, but he did move. Making the transition from one room to another didn't take a lot of work. He owned nothing but the clothes on his back—clothes that had been laundered twice since his arrival at the old folks' home—and a small bag of retirement home toiletries he'd been given as he left The Egg. He still thought that was a weird name for an old folks' home, but that's what everyone called it. Ivy had told him why, early on, but at the time he'd been so intent on her face and her voice he didn't remember many details of her explanation. *Gifted.* He remembered gifted.

He was happy to note the cooler temperature in the Bed and Breakfast, and even happier when the cute and weirdly happy proprietor led him to a ground floor room. Stairs wouldn't stop him, but they would damn well slow him down.

His room was much smaller than the apartment at The Egg, and though he didn't remember much of anything about himself, he did realize the decorating style wasn't what he normally preferred. There was a multi-colored quilt on the queen-sized bed, enough decorative pillows for half a dozen rooms, and a rocking chair that squeaked when he sat in it. The attached bathroom was tiny. Toilet, pedestal sink, clawfoot tub that had seen better days. There was a rise in the floor so that the door wouldn't close all the way. The walls were a bright pink, and the linoleum on the floor was cracked in a couple of places. The bathroom was so small, he almost had to step back into the bedroom in order to turn around.

But it wasn't a hundred degrees.

Door closed, toiletries stored in the bathroom medicine cabinet, Grant sat in the creaking rocking chair and closed his eyes. He'd need clothes soon, as well as new shoes to replace the sneakers that had been all but ruined in the river. Food had been provided at The Egg, and maybe would be provided here, but how long could he expect the town of Mystic Springs to support him? He needed a lot of things, everyday, normal things that he could think of, but he had no money to pay.

Over the past three days his head had cleared, somewhat. He still didn't remember shit, but he was able to think. Sitting here alone, in a room that wasn't intolerably hot, he took a deep breath and tried to focus.

Who would've shot him? Why? Even though he had no memory, he was pretty sure he wasn't a criminal. Maybe he just didn't want that to be true. Benedict would've arrested him by now if he was wanted anywhere. Had they taken fingerprints? Maybe while he was out. He was still pretty sure the police chief wouldn't have put him at The Egg if there was any chance he was a danger to the people there. All Benedict would need to do was look up Grant Whitlock on a law enforcement database and...

He jumped up, moving quickly for the first time in days. It only hurt a little bit, a good sign he was on the mend. He opened the door to his room and stepped into the hallway. The kitchen was down the hall to the right. He heard movement there and headed in that direction. Sure enough Molly was in the kitchen, preparing dinner.

"Hey," he called casually.

The innkeeper gasped and turned quickly, then smiled when she saw him standing there. "You startled me."

"Sorry. I was just wondering... do you have a computer?

Ivy spent all afternoon mulling over Luke's words, as she sold sweets and bread to customers. She didn't say much as she worked, but then she never did so no one seemed alarmed by her mood. They were used to her standoffish air, her inability to be truly friendly even with those who frequented her bakery and provided her with a decent living. It wasn't that she didn't have friends; she did. But she always felt a little separate, a little off, as if everyone else knew something she didn't. The secrets of life; the recipe for contentment. There were days she felt as if everyone was in on a joke she'd missed.

That said, she'd never felt as if she wasn't accepted here. She was. She was an important part of this town, and always would be. Imperfect as it was, this was her place in the world.

There had been a time when Luke Benedict's gift for knowing what people needed was limited to batteries and toilet plungers. Socks and postage stamps. If he told you that you needed something from his hardware store, you bought it then and there or regretted it later.

During the past year, his gift had shifted. Like everything else in Mystic Springs, it had changed. Grown. He could still tell you if you were going to need a light bulb, but he could also suggest other, more important things.

You need to see the doctor.

You need to apologize to your brother.

You need to leave him, now.

And in her case... *You need to listen to your heart. The fate of this entire town depends on it.*

She could see where the first part might apply, but what did her love life or lack thereof have to do with the fate of Mystic Springs?

Ivy closed up shop a little later than usual, packed a box of sweets, and locked up. Eve's Cafe was still hopping. On many an evening Ivy would head straight there after she closed her business, but not tonight. She still wasn't ready to face Eve, who would take one look at her face and start asking questions Ivy didn't want to answer. She took her box of goodies and started walking.

She loved autumn, and tonight was one of those spectacular cool evenings that everyone wished would last forever. There was a gentle breeze, and down the side streets and in the woods that surrounded their small town, leaves were taking on color. Not a lot, not yet, but the change had begun. Dark came a bit earlier in the evening, but at the moment there was enough light in the sky so she wasn't lost in darkness. Not that she'd ever been afraid of the dark. Eve, on the other hand...

Ivy didn't head for home, which is where she should've gone, but walked down another block, then right, then all the way to The Riverside Rest Bed and Breakfast.

The big white house wasn't literally on the river, but it was on the east side of town and about as close to the river as you could get and still be in Mystic Springs.

Her heart started pounding as she approached the front porch. She hadn't listened to that heart for a very long time, but if she listened now as Luke suggested, if she paid attention at all, it led her straight to Grant.

Tonight she wasn't just going to listen to her heart; she was going to take the advice of her good friend Marnie Maxwell.

CHAPTER 7

Grant sat at the dining room table and leaned over the ancient laptop Molly had loaned him. The device and the Wi-Fi were both crap. The computer kept flickering and going dark before coming to life again, always on a completely different page. Recipes, usually. Maybe that's what Molly used the laptop for most days.

His name was Grant Whitlock, he knew that much. At least, that's what he'd been told. He'd been in Mystic Springs before, and a few people remembered his name. Those few people remembered nothing else about him, at least not that they'd share. Nothing about his job, if he had one, his family… if he had one. Grant Whitlock wasn't all that unusual a name, but he found nothing but little kids and old men in his search.

He'd been so sure he'd learn something on the internet. Anything. Surely he had some kind of social media account. When he'd mentioned this to Molly she'd brushed it off and said she didn't have anything, either, that social media in general had gotten far too negative for her. She wasn't at all alarmed that there was no trace of him on the web, but he was. Did that make it more likely that he was a shady character? He'd dismissed that possibility, but who else would go to all the trouble it would take to hide from the world?

Someone should've reported him missing. What kind of man was he that no one, not a single soul, was concerned that he'd been gone for almost a week? What about the bride in the yellow sundress?

That image was the only one from his past that stuck with him. He kept expecting something else to emerge, but so far that was it. At least it was a pleasant image.

A dislike of cabbage and a faceless bride. That was all he knew about himself. It was frustrating to search his mind—and the internet—and find nothing.

Ivy arrived while he was trying, again, to discover something of himself on the internet. He'd had zero luck so far, but if he kept trying maybe something useful would appear on the screen. He couldn't give up now; there had to be *something*. A recipe for sourdough bread popped up and stayed for almost two seconds. Then it was gone.

Ivy carried another one of those purple boxes. He'd seen one just like it on the kitchen counter when he'd asked Molly about borrowing her computer. If he wasn't careful, he was going to put on so much weight while he was recovering. A man could only eat so many cupcakes without paying a price. He'd seen guys…

The thought came and went, started to make sense and then did not.

Ivy placed the box on the dining room table and asked, "What's this?"

Molly shrugged her shoulders. "Grant's trying to find himself online but so far he's not having any luck."

"This computer isn't exactly the best, and I think the Wi-Fi is wonky," he said.

"It is," Molly said. "It really is. I need to see about getting faster and more reliable service installed, but I'm afraid that's pretty far down the list as far as renovations go."

Grant slammed the laptop lid down and leaned back in disgust. It wasn't the slow internet or the crappy laptop that annoyed him, it was the fact that as far as he could tell, no one was looking for him. Not a wife, not a friend, not a co-worker. Was he so unimportant that he could vanish without a trace and no one cared enough to put out a "Have you seen this man?" Facebook post? How sad was that?

He looked into Ivy's face. In spite of the harsh set of her features, the view comforted him. She was beautiful but it was more than that. There was a hidden element on her face that only he could see. It soothed and excited at the same time; it spoke to him in a gut-deep way. He could only compare it to the secret ingredient in a special recipe. There was more to Ivy Franklin than met the eye.

He wanted to know what it was.

"Stay for dinner," he said.

Molly looked less than pleased that he'd invited Ivy to stay.

"There's enough, right?" he added, glancing at the innkeeper.

Suddenly Molly smiled, much too widely. "Sure. More than enough. Ivy's welcome to stay, as long as she doesn't have, you know, a date or something. I know Doctor Levi has asked her out more than once."

Ivy looked annoyed. Well, more annoyed than usual. "Does everyone know everything in this town?"

Molly shrugged casually, but somehow looked far too pleased with herself. Grant felt like someone had told a joke he didn't get. He glanced at Ivy, trying to judge the expression on her face, trying to picture her with Redmon. It was an image he didn't care for.

"I'm not dating Levi or anyone else," she snapped. "And if I was, it wouldn't be anyone's business but mine."

Grant was washed in an emotion that could only be called

relief. He didn't want this beautiful redheaded baker he barely knew dating anyone. He wanted her all to himself.

~

Bria was less adventurous than Felicity. It was just her nature, Felicity told herself, not truly a character flaw.

The shyer girl needed a friend to encourage her to do things she might otherwise not even attempt. Bria needed to be drawn out of her shell, and Felicity was trying to do just that. It was her duty as a BFF.

It was necessary, for their families, their friends… their world.

"I didn't know he was going to get shot," Bria whispered as together, the two girls peeked through the B&B dining room window.

"It's not like he died," Felicity argued. "And just look! Isn't this how it's supposed to be? We did a good thing."

"Maybe," Bria muttered.

Ivy sat at the dining room table across from Grant Whitlock. He was fascinated with her, you could tell by the way he stared at her when she wasn't looking. That had to be love, right? He had to care. On occasion Ivy actually smiled. Smiled! She always caught herself after a moment or two, the smiles didn't last long, but they were real. They were a start of something new and exciting.

This town desperately needed new and exciting.

Satisfied that their plan was underway, the girls stepped away from the window and started walking toward home.

"We should ask for help," Bria said. "We're too young to do this on our own."

"In the old days some women got married at thirteen," Felicity argued.

"It's not the old days," Bria mumbled.

"We're more powerful than any of the other witches in town,

but that won't last long if we don't do something. Imagine it, once this is done we'll be able to go anywhere we want and take our magic with us. We can go to college in a few years without leaving what makes us special behind." She looked at her friend. "We'll find a permanent solution to your ghost problem, I swear it."

Poor Bria, she saw ghosts at the most inopportune times! As if there was ever a good time to see a ghost. Their great-grandmothers had fashioned a talisman that usually kept the ghosts at bay, but it didn't always work.

Felicity really wanted another look at the book that had led them to this point, but the library was closed and she didn't want to raise any alarms by breaking in and maybe getting caught. The library was closed on Sunday. If she called Ms. Marnie and asked to be let in, the librarian would happily comply. Book lovers stuck together.

Yes, she could get into the library tomorrow, but how would she explain her request? And how would she keep the librarian away from the book? Ms. Marnie was notoriously nosy. It was always best if there were others in the library when they wanted to study a book in that section.

Felicity didn't want to wait until Monday, but she would. Patience might be a virtue, but it was so hard!

Besides, she remembered the important parts. She remembered the passage that had set this plan in motion.

At the fall of Ivy, when the stars align, the protections that isolate Mystic Springs from the rest of the world might finally disappear.

What could that possibly mean, other than Ivy falling in love? If there were cliffs nearby, or tall buildings, maybe they'd have to consider other possibilities. But there weren't. This part of Alabama was really, really flat, so the only fall Ivy might experience was... love.

This was important. Nothing could stop them now! One day she and Bria were going to take a trip and see real mountains.

The Rockies, maybe. She'd seen pictures but she wanted to be there in person, and with her magical abilities at full strength.

The plan was moving forward. Full steam ahead! When Ivy fell in love, she and everyone else in Mystic Springs would finally be free.

~

Dinner was good, though Molly wasn't exactly the most cordial host. She'd said earlier in the day that her new—and only—boarder was cute. Studly. Did she have plans for him herself? Did she see Ivy as competition?

Of course she did. Who was she to complain? It had been Molly's obvious interest that had spurred Ivy to take a chance. To seek out Grant and what they might have. Temporarily, at least.

Spending time close to Grant was wonderful, at times, but it was also more difficult than she'd imagined it would be. She liked her life neat and tidy, with no surprises or variations from routine. This was a definite variation. She remembered what he did not. The love. The tough decision to let him go. The heartbreak she'd never been able to shake, no matter how she tried. The wedding.

No one who knew her would accuse Ivy Franklin of being subtle. Not as a child, not as an adult. She grabbed what she wanted; she took no prisoners and brooked no nonsense. She said what was on her mind, no matter what the consequences might be.

She'd been indecisive all week, but the time for caution was over. She knew what she wanted, and she was going to take it.

When dinner was over and a sullen Molly had cleared the table and disappeared into the kitchen, Ivy stood. When she was on her feet, Grant stood, too. The table was between them. The table and five years and a bullet wound and... so many things. She should wait, play things safe, take it slow.

But that had never been her way.

"Where's your room?" she asked.

Grant's eyebrows lifted slightly. He smiled and said, "Right this way."

His room was on the ground floor, which was good for him as he healed but maybe not so good in other ways. The kitchen where Molly banged pots and pans was right down the hall, much too close. Molly's own room, if she'd taken the one her aunt had once called her own, was two doors away. Also too close. And too convenient, given that the innkeeper was obviously taken with Grant.

The location of his room was not ideal, but it would do for now.

He opened the door and stepped inside. It was a small room, Ivy noted, too feminine and old-fashioned for his tastes. Shoot, it was too feminine for her! There were too many doodads, too many bright colors and pillows. She'd never gotten the decorative pillow thing.

She followed Grant into the room and closed the door behind her. After a moment's consideration, she locked it.

He looked a little surprised, but not shocked, exactly. Surely he felt the chemistry between them. She'd kissed him before, had even slept in his bed. No, he should not be surprised. Was that surprise or was it... anticipation? Memories or no, he experienced some of the same emotions and desires she did.

She walked into his arms, lifted her head without hesitation, and kissed him. Even though he didn't remember her, she remembered him. She remembered *this*. The warmth of his lips. The way he tasted and smelled. The way the rest of the world melted away when they were alone. He didn't remember that, he couldn't, but nothing about the way he kissed her had changed. It was instinctive. Natural. Inevitable. They came together not like people who'd just met, but like lovers who'd been apart for too long.

It was so easy to fall into him, to forget everything but the way he made her feel. The kiss was fine, it was glorious, but it wasn't enough. She wanted skin to skin contact; she wanted him to be a part of her, the way he'd once been. Maybe in the end she'd just have to send him away all over again, but for now, in this moment, he could be hers.

She could be happy.

Grant sat on the side of the bed and pulled her down to sit beside him. They continued to kiss, to meld together, to melt toward the inevitable end. He moved, and the bed squeaked. Loudly. Ivy didn't care. Let Molly hear, let her know that Grant was taken.

He was hers. He always had been.

Ivy couldn't wait any longer for *more*. She unbuttoned Grant's shirt and touched his chest. The kiss deepened; he wanted her as much as she wanted him, she could feel it. He slipped his hand up her thigh, under her skirt, to brush her where she was already throbbing for him.

They'd come together easily five years ago, and they came together easily now. If it was truly possible that one human could be made for another, he was hers. She was his. Ivy wasn't known to be such a hopeless romantic, but the thought did cross her mind.

In spite of what Luke had said about following her heart, she wasn't here for romance; she was here for sex. Passion and physical need were much easier to accept, to embrace. Love was... messy. Unpredictable. Complicated. It would be easy enough for Luke to confuse sex and love, she told herself. Men did that all the time.

She refused to take the other part of Luke's advice seriously. How could her love life have any effect on the town? Even Luke Benedict was allowed to have an off day, she supposed.

Her hand went to the zipper of Grant's jeans. Yes, he wanted her, the evidence was clear. She wouldn't pretend to be shy; coy wasn't her way. She was ready to climb on top of him and ride him until they both had what they wanted, until she screamed at the ceiling. Nothing could stop this. Her entire body throbbed. It had been so long since she'd wanted anything so badly, since this power had overtaken her

Love. Passion. A desire that was strong enough to make everything and everyone else disappear.

Grant's hand settled over hers, stilled her movement. He turned his head, pulled his lips from hers and took a deep breath.

"I can't," he whispered.

"Oh, shit, your wound! I thought it was healing pretty well..."

"That's not it." He looked her in the eye, and she could see the desire mixed with pain. Not physical pain, but something deeper. "I want you. I feel... something powerful between us, something strong and unexpected. But I can't."

Again, those words. "I think you can." She knew he wanted her. That was a fact he couldn't hide.

"No, I can't," he said again. "I can't explain it, but I think I'm married."

CHAPTER 8

Ivy held her breath for a long moment. Before Grant had been found here just days ago, she'd paid enough attention to his life to know that he wasn't married. Not unless you counted their unofficial, undocumented, not at all legal, spur of the moment wedding.

Which he could not possibly remember.

She found her voice after a long pause, and as calmly as she could manage asked, "What makes you say that? Are your memories coming back?"

Impossible. Terrifying. At least he didn't seem to have a clue that the *wife* he kinda sorta remembered was her.

Grant backed away from her a little. He seemed to be reluctant to separate, but who could know? Maybe she was reading all the signals wrong. Maybe he didn't really want her after all. The amnesia punch might've well and truly wiped her from his mind. It should've. Was it possible this wonderful moment, the passion that had overwhelmed her, was... one-sided? That would be embarrassing.

A part of her wanted to bolt from the bed and run. She'd tried and failed. No matter what the cause, she'd just been rejected.

Grant raked a hand through his hair, making it stand more on end than usual. "I still don't remember anything. Not my name, where I'm from, how I got here, who would've shot me. There's just one maddeningly indistinct visual memory that keeps popping up when I least expect it. Like now."

"A memory of what?" she snapped.

"A bride in yellow, walking down a church aisle toward me." His voice was much calmer than her own; he was in complete control. "I can't see her face and that's driving me crazy, but I know it was a wedding, and... I know I love her, whoever she is."

She's me!

She couldn't say that, so she bit back the words that were on her lips. "Whoever this bride was, or is, why isn't she looking for you? You've been here almost a week, and there's been nothing on the news, no *Have You Seen This Man?* stories."

"I know," he said. There was the frustration she'd been experiencing, in his voice. "That's what I was trying to find on the computer when you got here, but that computer is next to worthless."

As if they could allow Non-Springers unimpeded internet access...

Best not to go there... "Maybe you're remembering wrong."

"I don't think so," Grant whispered.

If the memory ever intensified, if it grew clearer and he realized she was the bride, would he be relieved or angry? Both, maybe. She hadn't thought things could get any worse, but if Grant hated her she couldn't bear it.

She wasn't glib, she'd never been able to talk her way out of anything. That was a trait her twin possessed, but not her. Was it possible she could give it a go? Could she manage to talk her way out of this mess?

"Could be a scene from a movie you're remembering," she said, her voice deceptively casual. "Maybe you were at that wedding as a guest and the visual stuck with you."

"I don't think so." He looked her in the eye. "I like you a lot. I'm drawn to you. I want you, I do. There's something about you gets under my skin in a way that's maddening and yet feels so right. It's hard to define. But the bride I see in my dreams and in my waking hours, I love her. I feel it in my gut, in my soul. That certainty hits me deep, every time."

"She's not here," Ivy argued. Love the one you're with, right? Wasn't that supposed to be the way?

"No, but she's *here*." Grant placed a hand over his heart.

Ivy's heart broke. For him, for herself, for all the bad decisions she'd made. She'd tried to deny it but she loved him, too, and had since the moment she'd seen him. She'd been a fool to think she could cast him out and start over, that she might find love again with another man. She'd been even more of a fool to think she could just sleep with him and move on.

She hadn't realized how precious their love was, how rare and pure. It could not be replaced or recreated, not for her.

They loved each other, but he didn't understand.

And she couldn't tell him.

~

Grant lay on top of his bed hours after Ivy had departed as if the devil was on her tail. He couldn't blame her. To come so close and then be rejected...

What kind of an idiot turned down a woman like Ivy Franklin? He imagined she was the one who did the rejecting in her relationships. Like she had with the doc, apparently.

He wanted her. They had a strong connection of some kind. Sex with her would be out of this world. When she'd asked where his room was he'd been willing and able. Sitting on the bed kissing her, he'd been swept away. For a few precious minutes he'd set everything else aside. He hadn't cared who shot him, that he had no memory, that no one in the world seemed to be looking for him.

But when he'd touched Ivy, when she'd touched him and they'd been seconds away from being naked, he'd been hit with a vivid image of his bride in yellow. It had been so strong it was like an assault on his brain; the woman in yellow would not be denied. The image had hit him like a speeding truck and bowled him over. More than the mental picture was the intense sensation of love that had washed over him. Hard to say, with no fucking memory, but he was pretty sure he'd never felt that way about anyone else but his bride. That was a once in a lifetime love.

He didn't know who his bride in yellow was, or where she was, but she wasn't a figment of his imagination. He hadn't manufactured her out of thin air. She was real, and no matter how much he wanted to, he wouldn't betray her. Not even with a woman like Ivy.

The bride was his anchor to the real world, the one thing he could hold onto as he waited for his memories to return. What if they didn't? What if that one maddening image was all he had? As soon as he was able, he'd find her. He'd search the world over, if he had to. Someone beyond this little town would be able to help him. The alternative was too devastating to consider.

Sleep didn't come easy, but it did come. He'd gone to sleep hoping to dream of his bride and maybe see more detail this time, but he didn't. He dreamed of uncooperative computers and strawberry cupcakes he couldn't quite reach. Yet more frustration. At two in the morning, according to his bedside clock that glowed red in the dark, a howl from outdoors but far too close for comfort awakened him.

A minute later, something—or someone—scratched at his window.

He considered getting up to investigate, but then thought better of it. It had to be a branch brushing against the window.

Was there a tree right outside the window? Had it gotten windy? The sound came again, a slow scraping sound. Grant threw back the covers, walked to the window, and drew back the thick curtains.

No tree. No person. No animal. It hadn't been his imagination, dammit, but nothing was there.

Movement caught his eye. In the middle of the backyard an animal of some kind peered around a dilapidated garden fence. He couldn't tell what kind of animal it was, maybe a really big dog. Were there bears around Mystic Springs? Coyotes, maybe, though he didn't think they got that big.

While he pondered, a trick of the moonlight made the animal's eyes glow red.

Grant dropped the curtain and crawled back into the bed. Sleep didn't come again for a very long time.

On Monday morning, Ivy was shocked to see Grant walk through the bakery door. Great. He moved a little awkwardly, a little slowly, but he didn't have a cane or a walker. He'd probably rather fall flat on his face than use either.

She'd spent all day Sunday talking herself out of going to him and telling him everything, convincing herself that he'd be gone soon enough and her life could get back to normal. Happiness was overrated, anyway. Felicity and Bria were too young to have any idea what happiness truly was. It was complicated, elusive, and all too often came with a hefty price. All anyone could hope for were moments of happiness spread throughout their lives. She'd had hers.

As for Marnie's advice to sleep with Grant… well, she'd tried. No need to make a fool of herself by trying again.

"What do you want?" she snapped as Grant approached the glass case.

Instead of being put off by her attitude, he smiled. "Good morning, Grant. How nice to see you on this fine morning. What can I do for you?"

"What do you want?" she asked again with a little less heat.

"Good morning to you, too, Ivy. The sun is shining and I just had to get out for a walk. The doc says it'll be good for me to move. Those cupcakes look delicious. So do the blueberry scones. What do you recommend?"

She sighed. He was tough to rattle. "The cinnamon rolls are especially good today."

He glanced past her to the coffeemaker. "I'll take two and a cup of coffee. Black."

With that he headed for one of the white wrought iron tables that were scattered about her place. Why couldn't he just get what he wanted to go and eat at the B&B? Molly would love to join him, she was sure. Even though she'd tried to distance herself emotionally, that certainty rankled. She couldn't have Grant for herself, but she sure as hell didn't want bubbly Molly to have him.

"Didn't Molly feed you this morning?"

"Yeah, but her egg casserole wasn't very good, the muffins were full of nuts, and she was in a worse mood than you are." He very carefully lowered himself into a chair.

Impossible! No one was in a worse mood than she was. Especially today.

As she approached his table with the cinnamon rolls and coffee, he looked up and said, "I was wondering if you know of another place I could stay while I'm in town. I'm sure I have money somewhere, and eventually I'll be able to pay. The jeans and sneakers I was wearing might've been covered with mud and soaked with river water, but they weren't cheap. Even I can tell that much." He looked into her eyes. "Maybe I could get a job to hold me over. Do you need any help? I can't cook, at least I don't think I can, but I can sweep and wash dishes."

"I do fine on my own, I don't need any help." She couldn't stop herself from asking, "What's wrong with the bed and breakfast? The Egg was too hot. Is the B&B too cold? What are you, Goldilocks?"

He looked a little uncomfortable as he took a sip of coffee, tore off a small piece of the cinnamon roll, and popped it into his mouth. His eyes lit up. "Holy cow, that's good."

Ivy sat across the table from him. "Don't change the subject. But thanks," she added. "Why do you want to move?"

He leaned toward her. "Is Molly a good friend of yours?"

"Nope."

"I get a weird vibe from her."

"A weird vibe," Ivy repeated. "It's simple enough, really. She likes you, a lot I think, and if you've told her you're being faithful to your imaginary bride..."

"My bride's not imaginary," he said defensively.

"Whatever."

"There's more. For the past two nights, some kind of animal has been howling out back and scratching at my window."

Her heart leapt, a little. The Milhouses had been out in force over the weekend, but they usually stuck to the outskirts of town. Why would they harass Grant? Maybe it was something else. Or someone else. "What did this animal look like?"

Grant shook his head. "I tried to get a good look Saturday night, but I was too late. Whatever it was had moved into the back yard. All I could see was what looked like a... a big dog, maybe." He hesitated, took a sip of coffee. "Might've been a trick of the light, but the thing looked like it had red eyes. I don't think that's possible."

"And last night?" Ivy prodded.

"Last night, I didn't bother to check."

She smiled. "Did you hide your head under the covers and wait for it to go away?"

He popped another piece of the sweet into his mouth. "Pretty

much." Then he added. "Nice smile. You should use it more often."

Grant looked out the front window, grimaced a little, and took a slow sip of coffee. "Maybe I should just move on. I don't have a thing to my name, but I can hitchhike to a bigger town, find some kind of a job, go to a police station where they have more than one cop on duty and ask for help. Everyone here has been great, don't get me wrong, but… I need to know." He looked at her, then. "I need to find her."

Ivy knew what she had to do, what she needed to do, but when she was this close to Grant, when she looked into his eyes, every instinct within her screamed *mine*. She wanted him, this one last time. He was hers, she loved him still, and she'd be damned if she'd hide a moment longer.

Somehow she had to convince Grant to cheat on her. With herself. If she sent him away again before she took that chance, she'd regret it for the rest of her life.

She reached over and plucked off a small piece of his cinnamon roll. "Don't leave just yet. If you just head out without a plan there's no telling what you'll find. I have a spare bedroom. You're welcome to it, if you think that would suit you better than the B&B."

He looked surprised. "Are you sure?"

She supposed it was unusual for a woman who'd been sent packing when she was halfway to paradise to invite the man who'd done the sending to move in with her. Most women gave up more easily than Ivy. "Why not?"

After a short hesitation Grant accepted her offer.

Let the games begin…

CHAPTER 9

Ivy's house wasn't exactly what he'd imagined. There was a warmth to it that didn't suit the persona she presented to the world. Here, in her home, she let the best of herself shine through. It wasn't cluttered like the B&B, though there were a few knick-knacks here and there. The walls were painted a warm peach; no generic white for Ivy. On a shelf filled with books there was a figurine, a woman holding a loaf of bread, that looked pretty old. Maybe it was a family doodad.

A single pillow on the couch, more utilitarian than decorative. An afghan over the back of that couch. A few small houseplants, all well cared for.

There weren't a lot of pictures, but he saw a few. Most were of Ivy and her twin. There was one old framed photo of a family of four. Mother, father, twin red-headed girls. For some reason, that photo made him sad. Maybe because there were no more recent photos of that complete family.

He realized, had seen from the start, that Ivy's toughness was false. She wore her I-Don't-Care attitude the way a kid might wear a Halloween costume. He wasn't sure why he knew that without doubt, but he did. Maybe here, in this small home filled with warm colors and small comforts, she let the real Ivy shine through.

The guest bedroom she showed him to was smallish, and the bathroom he'd be using was across the hall, but still, he liked it better than his old-fashioned room at the bed and breakfast. The decor was simple, the colors soothing blues and greens. There were no decorative pillows, not even one. The window faced the street, so maybe no animals from the woods that surrounded the town would venture to it. A painting over the bed was an impressionist style, people on a busy street. Maybe the colors she'd used in decorating had been chosen to compliment the painting.

He was instantly more comfortable here than he'd been at The Egg or the B&B. Was it the place or the hostess? He suspected the latter to be true.

Molly had been initially annoyed when he'd told her he was moving on, but that annoyance hadn't lasted long. In fact, by the time he'd walked out the front door, she'd seemed almost glad to be rid of him.

He wasn't entirely sure why he'd gone straight to Ivy's bakery this morning. They hadn't exactly parted on the best of terms. In fact, their last meeting had been beyond awkward. It would've made more sense to go to the doctor for help, or to Chief Benedict. One of them could help him find another place to stay, get a job, simply move on to another town. Benedict could drive him up the road and he'd make his way from there. He still had no memory of his past, but he wasn't helpless. There had to be a main road, a bigger town, people who had internet that worked.

If Molly was right and Doc Redmon had a thing for Ivy, he might be very glad to help Grant move elsewhere. Anywhere but here...

There was no denying that he'd been drawn to Ivy since the beginning. Yeah, he'd sent her packing before he could cheat on the wife he could barely remember. It hadn't been easy, but he'd made himself stop things before they'd gone too far. But still, he had a connection to Ivy. There was something inexplicable between them. Why fight it?

He placed his small bag of stuff on top of a dark chest of drawers then headed to the kitchen, where Ivy waited for him.

"Sorry you had to close up early on my account," he said.

"Mondays are usually slow. And besides, I close whenever I feel like it. No one will care."

If he headed there for a treat of some kind and found her bakery closed he'd care, but he didn't tell her so. "Well, I appreciate it. You can head back there, if you want. I need to check in with the doctor this afternoon, and somehow I need to round up some clothes. These have been washed a few times since I came to town, but a spare anything would make my life a lot easier." He didn't need much, but clean socks, underwear, maybe a couple of t-shirts and another pair of jeans. The shoes were in bad shape, thanks to the river water, but they'd do. For now. "I guess I need a job, though I'm not sure what I can do at this point."

Ivy rolled her eyes. "You do not need a job. Not now, anyway. You need to heal first. Priorities, Whitlock," she snapped. "Priorities."

"Maybe by the time you deem me ready to work I'll remember who I am. Surely I already have a job." Somewhere...

She glared at him, then cast his way a uniquely Ivy expression of disdain. For some weird reason, he liked it. There it was, that Halloween costume.

"We can round up some clothes for you," she said. "They might not be what you're accustomed to..."

He smiled. "But since I don't remember what I'm accustomed to that doesn't matter much."

"When you feel up to it we'll head back to town. The antiques store has a thrift shop section in the back. They usually have some old clothes, maybe shoes in your size, if we're lucky." Her expression softened. "I'm almost certain you'll find what you want there."

He was more and more certain that what he wanted was right here.

~

Sure enough, everything Grant needed was in the used clothing section at the back of the antiques store. The owner had a Benedict among her ancestors, though it was a couple of generations back. That came in handy, now and then.

Grant gravitated to the shirt rack. Ivy went to the shoes and then to a shelf that had underwear and socks, and a couple sets of men's pajamas. When she presented what she'd found to him he turned up his nose at it all, and suggested that she return the PJs. He said he was pretty sure he didn't wear them.

"You're not running around my house in your underwear," Ivy said in a low but sharp voice that left no room for argument. *Or naked,* though she didn't say that out loud.

She paid for his purchases. He protested, but what the hell else was he going to do? It wasn't like the necessities they purchased cost all that much.

When they left the antiques store they headed for the doctor's office. Levi would have to tell her if she needed to do anything to care for the wound on Grant's side. As far as she could tell it was healing nicely. He moved well, with just the occasional hitch in his step. Maybe the quick healing was due to luck, or his superb physical condition. Then again, maybe it was Mystic Springs itself. He'd been shot a week ago. Shouldn't he be limping? Wincing? Complaining?

Maybe he walked a bit too slowly, but that was it as far as allowances for the injury went.

It wasn't her imagination that people stared as she and Grant walked by. They all knew who he was, and they'd been told not to let him in on the secret. No one would know that he'd be staying with her for a while, not yet, and none of them knew how much she'd loved him, or that she planned to seduce him very shortly then send him on his way. That would wipe him out of her system. That would put him in his place.

And if it didn't...

Levi was with a patient, but there was no one in the waiting room except for Ivy and Grant. Ivy squirmed in her chair. Levi needed to hire a receptionist one of these days. He had a part time nurse's aide who only worked a couple afternoons a week. The other days she worked at a clinic in Eufaula. The aide, who was yet another new resident of Mystic Springs, was never here when she was needed. Levi kept saying he needed to hire a receptionist and a nurse, but he never did. Pickings were slim, he said. It wasn't like there were a lot of Springers looking for work, and it wouldn't be smart to hire someone from out of town.

Janie Holbrook left the exam room area, a spring in her step and a smile on her face. She nodded to Ivy and winked at Grant, then headed out the door.

Ivy glanced at the once-sad plant sitting on the receptionist's desk. It looked much healthier than it had last week, greener, with new growth and longer stems. Janie must've whispered an encouraging word to the plant as she'd walked past.

It was just a couple of minutes before Levi stepped into the doorway and called Grant back. Ivy rose to accompany him. She needed to know if there was anything she was supposed to do. He'd be staying with her for a while which made him her responsibility. He was still on antibiotics, right? How long would he be taking them, and were there other medications he needed? Did she need to change his bandage? What were his limitations?

She really hoped there were none. Even though he'd rejected her once, she wasn't one to surrender easily. To anyone or anything.

Ivy hovered as Levi checked Grant's wound, in the same room where he'd been treated a week ago. She wanted a good look. No, it wasn't her imagination that he was healing extraordinarily well. Magic or a product of his overall health? Maybe both. In any case, if they were very careful there was nothing to keep them from having sex. She'd be on top, to save him the effort. Just thinking about it made her quiver a little.

No man should have the power to make her quiver, to crave. She craved *nothing*.

Nothing but Grant. He was a weakness. Her only weakness.

As Levi re-bandaged Grant's side, he said, "I'll stop by the B&B tomorrow morning before work and..."

"I'm not there anymore," Grant interrupted. "I'm staying with Ivy. She has a spare room."

Levi looked surprised, then disapproving. "Why is that?"

Grant looked at her, caught her eye. He didn't want the doctor to know everything. The attentions of an innkeeper; scratches at his window; a red-eyed animal. He probably also didn't want his doctor to know that Ivy had done her best to jump his bones and had been rebuffed.

Good thing she wasn't easily offended. It had been hard, having him turn her away, but there was nothing to keep her from trying again.

She said, "I'm going to hire him to do a little work around the bakery. I know he can't do much, but he needs to stay busy and earn a little cash while he's here. Until his memory comes back," she added. Once Grant knew he was a multi-millionaire, with two houses, three cars, and a fat bank account, he wouldn't be sweeping flour off her kitchen floor. Or sleeping in her guest bedroom. "It just makes sense for him to stay with me."

It didn't, not really, but he hadn't given her a lot of time to come up with a cover story.

Redmon seemed to be thinking. "Maybe I can stop by your house tomorrow after work."

"Why don't we just make an appointment in a day or two and I'll bring him by?" The last thing she needed was Levi Redmon hanging around while she was trying to seduce Grant.

Levi reluctantly agreed, and they set up a two-o'clock appointment for Wednesday afternoon.

As they left the office and headed back toward home, Ivy carrying Grant's "new" things in a plastic shopping bag, Grant leaned down toward her and said, in a lowered voice, "Molly was right. The doc has a crush on you."

"Well, I don't have a crush on him," she said sharply.

Grant looked far too pleased at those words.

The walk hadn't been arduous, but Grant was ready to sit by the time they got back to Ivy's house. Nothing in this town was very far away, at least not that he'd seen. There was the one downtown street where all the businesses seemed to be located, with homes close by on side streets that didn't seem to go very far. Ivy walked everywhere. So did everyone else. A block here, a couple of blocks there…

But he'd been shot a week ago, and even though he was healing well, he *had* been shot.

Ivy walked with him to his room, where she dropped his bag of purchases on the bed. "I have some out of season clothes in that closet, but there's plenty of room and some extra hangers, if you want to hang your shirts. Just push everything else back and make some space."

"For my three used shirts?"

"And your pajamas," she added.

Even though he remembered next to nothing he was pretty sure he didn't wear pajamas, but Ivy had insisted.

Now and then she passed by too closely, she brushed her hand on his arm, she stood so close he could feel her body heat. If he didn't know better he'd think she was doing it on purpose. He'd told her about his bride, that he was sure he was married and faithful. And yet, here she was.

He had to be honest with himself. When he'd decided to leave the B&B he could've gone to someone else. It didn't have to be Ivy, but then again… maybe it did.

He'd chosen her; she'd accepted him. And he was glad. This woman he barely knew had quickly and completely worked her way under his skin. He was obsessed with her; he wanted her. When she was around, he couldn't take his eyes off of her. The memory of a faceless bride had stopped him last time. Would it stop him again? Could he put that bride—imaginary or real, who knew—aside to have what he craved from this woman?

Memory or no memory, he was pretty sure most women who'd been turned down when they were minutes away from being naked would carry a grudge. Ivy didn't seem to remember, or care.

Here he was, living in her house, choosing her over all the other options, slim as they were, available to him. What the hell had he been thinking? Ah, he hadn't been. Instinct had driven him to her.

"Dinner in an hour," she said as she left the room and closed the door behind her.

For a while Grant sat on the bed with his back against the pillows and just rested. He needed to catch his breath. This mattress was better than the ones he'd slept on in the past week. The Egg bed had been like a rock. The mattress at the B&B had been so soft it had been too easy to sink into. This one was just right; it was easy to get comfortable here.

His mind constantly went to what might come next. He couldn't stay with Ivy indefinitely. Staying more than a day or two wouldn't be a good idea. It would make the most sense to ask Benedict to take him to the next town over, where he could start the search for his bride—and for himself—in earnest.

But he didn't want to leave Ivy. Was it possible to love two women at once? It was insane to even think of love with a woman he'd just met, but the thought came too naturally.

Eventually he left the bed and started unpacking. The underwear and socks, and the blasted pajamas, he stored in the top drawer of the chest by the door. He took his new shirts out of the bag, opened the closet door, and grabbed three hangers. One after another, he carefully placed each shirt on a hanger and hung them on the rack. When all three were there, he pushed the clothes to his right back a bit. Not because he needed the room but because the idea of the thrift store shirts touching Ivy's pretty dresses was an unpleasant one.

As he pushed against the dresses, colors flashed. She seemed to go out of her way to be dour at times, but there were bright colors hanging in her closet. Red, orange, purple, blue, green… yellow.

The flash of yellow caught his eye, and almost instinctively he moved the other dresses and blouses and skirts out of the way, sliding the hangers toward him, clearing a space so he could see clearly.

The yellow sundress hung almost at the back of the small closet, hidden from view. *Almost* hidden. Maybe Ivy had forgotten it was here. Maybe she'd completely forgotten the simple dress. In the shadows Grant couldn't be sure that garment was what he thought it was, so he grabbed the hanger and pulled it out.

The room swam so hard he grabbed onto the rack before him in order to remain standing. In his other hand he tightly gripped the hanger that held the summery yellow dress that swung there. It wasn't any yellow dress, it was *the* yellow dress. The one his bride had worn. The one Ivy had worn when she'd walked down the aisle toward him.

He wasn't in love with two women, wasn't torn at all. There was just one woman for him. Ivy.

The memory came back to him with a vengeance, and with such power it almost knocked him off his feet. He could see it all now. Ivy's face, that beautiful red hair, the smile she wore for him and him alone, the wildflowers they'd picked together for her bouquet. She'd said, "I do," and so had he. She'd become his wife.

The memory grew more and more vivid, it took shape and solidified, and then he had another memory, of the wedding night. The intense love he'd experienced when he'd first found the memory returned, crashing over him. He hadn't realized anyone could love so deeply.

Ivy was his wife, or had been. At one point, he still wasn't sure how long ago, they'd loved one another madly. What had happened? Why hadn't she told him? What was she hiding?

Why the hell was she pretending to be a stranger?

He marched away from the closet, dress in hand, accusations on his lips, but he stopped before opening the door and storming into the hallway as he'd intended.

His brain was working against him, as it had been for the past week. He didn't know nearly enough. Were they still married? Divorced? Separated? He might think the memory of their wedding was a false one but it was so vivid, not just in color but in the intensity of his feelings for Ivy.

He'd loved her madly; he could feel it, still.

Ivy had some serious explaining to do, but since she thought it was okay to play games with him, perhaps he could return the favor.

CHAPTER 10

Levi stood in the shadow of an old oak tree at the edge of the yard and watched Ivy's house. The cover was unnecessary. If he wished to remain unseen, he would remain unseen. For now, extra caution was warranted. Caution didn't come naturally to him, but he had learned...

Even though the plan was proceeding as he'd intended, his pride was wounded. His ego had taken a blow. But as disturbing as it was, he couldn't let his ego get in the way.

Since coming back to Mystic Springs he'd tried everything to get Ivy to fall for him. He'd been excessively nice. He'd smiled even when it hurt his face to do so. When the opportunity arose, he cast sickeningly moony eyes in her direction, hoping she'd notice and be flattered. Maybe even interested. He never pushed; he was so damned respectful it was nauseating. Wasn't that what women like Ivy wanted? A pushover. Someone to adore them and do their bidding.

For months he'd pursued her, for all the good it did him. Since she wasn't in a relationship and from all appearances hadn't been for a long while, he wrote off her reticence to a lack of interest in sex, in men in general. Still, he'd remained hopeful and persistent. For all the good it had done him.

He'd discovered a useful magic in the past few months. With a little effort, he could slip into the mind of a weak person and convince them to think the way he wanted them to. They never knew he was there, digging around in their thoughts, substituting his wants and desires for their own, filling their heads with his ideas.

Unfortunately, Ivy wasn't a weak-minded person. She'd continued to be uninterested in the opposite sex no matter how hard he tried to sway her.

This new plan had been a shot in the dark, a last minute effort. He hadn't been sure it would work at all, but he had to try something before it was too late. It had worked too well, and he didn't know whether to be relieved or annoyed. So he was both.

When Grant Whitlock had come back to town in such a dramatic way, Ivy Franklin had all but dropped to her back and spread her legs. It was what he'd hoped for but at the same time… maddening. What had he done wrong? What could he have done differently? He'd been so sure it wouldn't take long to sweep the pretty, lonely baker off her feet, mental manipulation or not. He'd been wrong. He hated to be wrong!

Plan A would've been much preferable to this messy Plan B, but… here they were.

His Granny Theodosia had been telling him for years that Ivy was the key. For a very long time he hadn't understood, or cared. He'd let her ramble, but had paid little attention to her words. Mystic Springs was in his past, a dying place he'd left as a child. It wasn't until he'd returned to the town—at his grandmother's request—for a week's vacation that he'd realized what being a Springer really meant. What would've happened if he'd never returned, if Theodosia hadn't realized she didn't have much time left and felt the need to go home for a visit? He would've remained a passably good doctor, an ordinary man in an ordinary world. Coming home had been her dying request. He'd grudgingly done it, for her, but he'd been the one to reap great benefits.

When his magic had come to life after spending a mere two days here, he'd realized he couldn't leave it behind. A month later his grandmother was dead. Her dying words had shaken him. *If you want to take your magic with you into the world, Ivy must fall.* He'd asked for more information, for details. Fall how? Fall in love? That seemed too simple. Besides, as far as he could tell she'd been in love before. Nothing had changed back then. If it had, none of this would be necessary.

He was trapped here with abilities that were continuing to develop, and with a powerful urge to show the world what he could do.

Ivy Franklin falling in love had changed nothing. That only left the other kind of fall.

He was going to have to destroy her.

Frustrated as he was, Levi took comfort from the fact that so far this plan was progressing well. He'd taken Whitlock's memories, and the man wouldn't get them back until his doctor was damn good and ready to return them. He'd played the part of a caring, simple-minded doctor well, trying to hide his true self. There was no time for a leisurely courtship, no use in nudging Ivy and Grant toward the finish line. Only chaos would free the powerful man Levi was destined to become. He was going to enjoy creating that chaos until he got what he wanted and needed.

In the distance a she-wolf howled. Levi looked toward the woods between him and the river, and smiled.

Ivy went out of her way to prepare the simplest meal possible for Grant and herself. The time for impressing him with her culinary skills beyond baking would come. Maybe. Sometimes a simple meal fed the soul, and that's what she–and Grant–needed tonight. She usually kept some homemade soup in the freezer. She thawed and warmed that soup and made cornbread. It was one of her favorite fall meals, and easy enough for a woman who lived alone.

And always would, with this temporary exception.

She'd never seduced a man before. There had been a couple of serious boyfriends before Grant, and one horrible mistake after, but with them sex had just... happened. One step and then another, and then the inevitable. With Grant, it had been like riding a wave. Powerful, inevitable. A force of nature had swept them along.

This was more deliberate. He'd really thrown her for a loop by stopping her advances with his insistence that he was married. She'd wanted to say, "Yeah, to me!" But she hadn't. It would be best if that memory never came back. Nothing could come of it.

The kitchen table was set when she leaned into the hallway and called, "Dinner's ready!" A moment later, the door to the guest room opened. She was tempted to watch Grant make his way down the hall; watching him was never a chore, but instead she retreated into the kitchen and fumbled around with the few dirty dishes that sat in the sink.

"Smells good," Grant said as he sat at the small table set in a nook by a window that looked over the back yard. There was normally a nice view, at the end of the day. Ivy usually ate earlier, but the day had gotten away from her and it was now fully dark, but for the light of an almost full moon.

Three nights out of the month, Milhouses ran the woods and howled to their hearts' content. After tonight there would be a break, until the next full moon. It had probably been a Milhouse who'd scratched at Grant's window the past couple of nights, though they normally didn't come into town. Then again, who else could it have been?

Ivy was tempted to tell Grant to eat without her. At the moment she wasn't sure she could even swallow. There was a huge knot in her throat, and in her stomach. Her heart was beating much too hard. Grant had rejected her once before. Why did she think she could change his mind now?

Because she truly believed, against all logic, that somewhere in the back of his mind he had to remember her. He must be experiencing some of the turmoil that was turning her inside out. This kind of emotional storm couldn't be entirely one-sided. Could it?

She wasn't usually such a coward! It had been a long time; since Grant had been in her life, since she'd wanted any man, since she'd been so damned *torn*.

Taking a deep, calming breath, she left the sink and joined Grant at the table, sitting directly across from him. Close, but not close enough…

"Looks good," he said.

"It's just soup," she said in a deprecating manner which was really not at all like her.

"And cornbread." Grant reached for a piece and placed it on the small plate beside his full soup bowl. Then he stopped, lifted his head, and looked at her. He looked at her *hard*.

She stared right back. No one made her flinch or look away, not even this man. "Is something wrong?"

"I don't know, Ivy," he said with a strange tinge of what might be suspicion in his voice. "Is something wrong?"

Where to begin…

She ignored the question, shrugged her shoulders, and started eating. Grant followed her lead and ate well. Thank goodness there was no chitchat during the meal. She did still plan to seduce him, but she really hoped that didn't include any small conversation. Just the sex would be fine, thanks very much.

Luke was wrong. Had to be. Her heart didn't need to be involved. Did she sometimes think she still loved Grant? Sure.

And in a way, in many ways, it was true. That didn't mean she could fool herself into thinking they had any chance of happily ever after.

Having Grant in Mystic Springs, and in her home, made her take an uncomfortable look at her life. She'd been hiding here; she couldn't deny that. She had her business, friends, family—a small but growing one, now that Eve was married and pregnant—and zero plans for the future. Her life was well-ordered, as ordinary as a Mystic Springs life could be. It would be possible to continue on this way until the day she died. Baking. Keeping a distance. Content in her solitude.

She was content, right?

In the distance, a Milhouse howled. Grant looked toward the window, but didn't seem alarmed. After all, he'd heard them the past two nights.

"Wild dogs," Ivy said as she stood, grabbing her empty bowl. "The area is lousy with them. That's probably what came to your window at the B&B." She placed her bowl in the sink. A wild dog made for an easier explanation than trying to explain away the local family of werewolves.

"Probably."

Ivy jumped; she hadn't realized Grant had left the table and was standing behind her. She turned around and found herself face to chest with the only man she'd ever loved. Having him so close made the realities of her intentions, such as they were, much more real.

Her body thrummed, the way it always had when he was near. Her insides quivered. No one else had ever made her feel this way. Why had she ever thought she could send him away and fall in love with someone else? There was no one else, not for her.

She was still trying to decide how to go forward. Should she be bold or coy? Coy was not her way, but she'd tried bold and it hadn't worked well. The idea that he might reject her again was enough to freeze her in her tracks. Fortunately she didn't have to make a single decision. Grant leaned in and down and kissed her.

He did know how to kiss. In an instant she was swept away. There was nothing but this; his mouth on hers, his hand at her waist, the thrum of blood through her body sweeping her away. No, not away, *to him.*

He ran a slow hand up her thigh, making Ivy wish she'd worn a skirt today. Still, the brush of his hand against her jeans was nice. More than nice, it was thrilling. That hand reminded her of so much. So much she'd lost, so much she'd thrown away.

Grant took his mouth from hers and lowered his lips to her neck. She almost came apart then and there, the sensations were so intense. She could melt. She could come here and now, with nothing more than his mouth there beneath her ear.

He lifted his head and whispered in her ear, "Maybe I do have a wife out there somewhere, but like you said, she's not here. You are. You're here."

He kissed her again, unsnapping her jeans and lowering the zipper. Wounded or not, the man could multitask. He slipped a hand into her open jeans, barely touched her where she was wet and ready for him. She gasped, moved her hips to give him better access, and answered the tongue he slipped into her mouth with a plunge of her own.

She was in heaven, but she was also unreasonably torn. This was exactly what she'd wanted, but… was Grant really so ready and willing to cheat on her? He'd said he loved his bride, but he didn't act like a man who cared about anything beyond… this. She forced that weird thought out of her mind, shut it down so she could enjoy the moment and the moments that were sure to follow. The jeans were nudged further down; his fingers moved deeper.

"If she was any kind of wife at all, she would've put the word out that I was missing." He followed that statement with his mouth on her throat; his finger slipped inside her. "Maybe she's dead," he whispered against her skin. "Maybe we're divorced. Maybe she just doesn't care anymore."

I care. She couldn't say that out loud.

The orgasm came fast and hard. She'd wanted to wait until he was inside her, until they were truly together, but he'd had other plans.

"Then again," Grant said as he removed his hand from her pants, "maybe I'm a disappointing husband who cheats whenever the spirit moves me, whenever a pretty girl flirts with me or hell, crosses my path."

"I'm sure you're not..." she began breathlessly, and then he slipped his hand to her back and unfastened her bra with a flick of his fingers. She stood before her kitchen sink, half undressed, still shaking, wanting more.

"You can't be sure of anything about me, can you?" Grant kissed her neck again. It was torture. It was heaven. "Is this the kind of thing you do all the time?" he asked, his voice oddly *cold*. "A strange man comes to town and you seduce him with cupcakes and cinnamon rolls and a kiss. Do you crawl into bed with every new guy that wanders into town, or..."

"Stop it." Tears filled her eyes and started to fall. She hated the tears, but she couldn't stop them. She wanted Grant, she needed him, but not like this. This was wrong, in a way she couldn't explain.

"Stop what?" he asked, stepping away, taking his mouth and his hands, his warmth and the promise of so much more.

"You're not a stranger," she whispered, and then she slipped past him and ran from the room.

CHAPTER 11

Grant heard Ivy's bedroom door slam. He was walking down the hall toward his own room when he heard the faint click of the lock.

He felt like an asshole, hell he *was* an asshole, but dammit, Ivy deserved a little payback. She'd lied to him. They hadn't been little lies, either. Not telling him that they were married, or had been, was a damn big omission.

Grant walked to the end of the hall, stood by her door for a few minutes trying to decide if he should knock or not. All the while he listened, wondering if he'd hear her crying or cursing. Either was possible, though she didn't strike him as a crier.

She was—or had been—his wife, so he should know for sure if she was a crier or not. From what little he knew of her, she probably threw and broke things when she was angry. That he could see all too well. The image of her walking down the aisle was vivid; he saw and felt that moment as if it had happened yesterday. The yellow dress pulled all the bits and pieces together. But he still remembered very little else, beyond that moment and snippets from the wedding night. He had no idea how they'd gotten to that church or what had happened since. He knew two things. He'd married Ivy. She'd lied.

It wasn't too late to call Benedict or Redmon and arrange another place to stay for the night. It wasn't even too late to get a ride out of town, to leave this all behind once and for all. But he didn't call anyone. He went to his room and closed the door.

And stared at the yellow dress.

Ivy wasn't the only one who'd lied. Someone else in this town had to know about the wedding. Some of them had surely been there! Small town weddings were a big deal, weren't they? Her sister surely knew, which meant Travis Benedict had to know. For the past week, they'd insisted that all they knew about him was his name.

Why would they lie about something like that? What kind of secrets did the residents of this little town keep? More than their share, he suspected.

He had a couple of choices, and the decision was an important one. He could get his ass out of town asap and start the search for his memories elsewhere. A bigger town, a better doctor.

Or he could stay and play the game, and find out what the hell was going on in Mystic Springs.

Ivy woke early, after a restless night, and headed to work as the sun was coming up. Like a coward, she'd tiptoed around the house being as quiet as possible so she wouldn't wake Grant. He'd know where she was, when he discovered she wasn't home. Would he care? That she didn't know. He'd been so angry last night, not at all like himself. She hadn't seen the anger coming, not after they'd kissed and he'd, well, she couldn't even think about it without shuddering. Best to put what had happened out of her mind.

Yeah, like that was going to work...

For all she knew, Grant wouldn't worry about her whereabouts at all. He might be in another state by the time she called it a day and headed home. All she knew was she wasn't ready to face him, not just yet.

She hadn't even made coffee in her own kitchen, afraid the noise or the aroma would wake her houseguest. She'd get her first cup at work, as she baked fresh goods for the day. Bread, for sure. Rolls. Dark chocolate cupcakes. Oatmeal raisin cookies.

Planning for the day should keep her mind off Grant, but it didn't. Her step was brisk as she walked a familiar sidewalk, trying her best to think of coffee and baking. It didn't quite work.

Ivy was so distracted by her wayward thoughts it was much too late to turn back when she saw her twin. Eve stood on the sidewalk near the door to the bakery. As she got closer, Ivy noticed the tense set to her twin's mouth. If she tried, just a little, she could feel the anxiety.

The baby.

Ivy crossed the street and broke into a jog. Something had to be wrong for Eve to be up so early and obviously waiting for her.

"You've been avoiding me all week," Eve said as Ivy approached, no longer running. Her tone was peevish, but not distressed or angry. So, *not* the baby. Thank God.

"I've been busy," Ivy said as she drew the key to her place out of her pocket and unlocked the door.

Eve made a dismissive noise and followed Ivy into the bakery. "Busy with Grant Whitlock, I hear."

"Your husband is a gossip."

"Please," Eve blew what seemed to be a disgusted puff of air between her lips. "As if Travis is the only one who knows what you've been up to. As if I can't *feel* the turmoil rolling off of you. Is Grant really living with you?"

Twin empathy aside, Eve always knew what was going on in Mystic Springs. People in her cafe talked, to her or to each other, and she always listened.

"He needed a place to stay," Ivy said as calmly as she could manage. "He's in the guest room."

For now.

Ivy slipped behind the glass case and started the coffeemaker.

Eve sat at a table near the case and sighed. "I remember very well how you felt about him, and how much it hurt when he went away."

"I sent him away, he didn't..." She couldn't finish that sentence. *He didn't choose to leave me. He didn't walk away. He didn't pick playing a game over me...*

Fortunately, with Eve she didn't have to say anything. Her twin knew.

Most people couldn't tell the Franklin twins apart. They were physically identical. If they'd wanted to one of them could've cut their hair differently, or added a pink streak or two. They could wear name tags or necklaces with their initials on them, but they didn't. Never had. Their parents had been able to tell them apart, and that was enough.

Travis had always been able to tell the difference between his wife and her twin. Of course he could...

They looked exactly the same, but their personalities were very different. Eve was outgoing, friendly, happy most of the time even before she'd fallen in love with Travis Benedict. Ivy was an introvert, occasionally unpleasant even before Grant had come into and gone out of her life, breaking her heart.

Eve cared too much. Ivy didn't care at all. At least, that's what she tried to tell herself.

When the coffee was ready—regular for her, decaf for Eve—Ivy carried two cups to the table where her twin sat and waited patiently. How much to tell?

At least where Eve was concerned, maybe honesty really was the best policy.

"You're right," Ivy said. "I've been avoiding you."

"Why? You can always talk to me about anything, any time. I

don't judge. I know how much he hurt you." Eve's expression softened. "I don't want to see it happen again."

"I still love him," Ivy said. "I wish I didn't. I've been trying to convince myself for days that it's not love, that it's just physical attraction, but I can't make it stick."

Eve sighed and reached a comforting hand across the table. Ivy didn't draw her own hand away, but let her twin's palm fall over her fist. The touch was nice, and was indeed comforting.

"There's something I never told you," Ivy said. She had to tell someone, had to share the burden. "I never told anyone."

Eve looked appropriately concerned. "I didn't think we had any secrets."

Ivy took a deep breath. "Just the one. When Grant was here before, I… I kinda married him."

Eve drew her hand away. Her expression was stunned, maybe even hurt. "How do you *kinda* marry someone? When? How? Why didn't you tell me?"

One question at a time…

"We went into Eufaula and had that old preacher at the Methodist Church perform the ceremony. His wife was the witness."

"Sounds solid enough to me," Eve muttered.

"I never filed the paperwork at the courthouse, so it's not legal. I just wanted… I wanted to say the words. It was a whim, an impulse. We were ready to be man and wife, we were…" *We were so much in love it hurt.* "Maybe deep inside I knew it wouldn't last. I told myself we could get married again later on, with you there, with friends and family. That ceremony was just for us, and…"

"What makes you think the preacher didn't file the paperwork?" Eve asked.

Horrors! "Why would he?"

"Did you tell him you didn't plan to do it yourself?"

"No. If I had, he probably wouldn't have agreed to perform the ceremony!"

"What if he checked, and thought it was an oversight, and... you said the wife was a witness. Was she a notary?"

Unthinkable... "I don't know. How can I find out for sure?"

"Marriage licenses are all in the public record, I think. I'll have Travis check."

"This is why I didn't tell you before," Ivy snapped. "You can't keep a secret! Travis will talk, he's a big ol' blabbermouth. Damn Benedicts. Once it gets back to Helen everyone in town will know."

Eve sighed again. "Remember, dear sister, I'm now a *damn Benedict.* Choose your words carefully."

"I notice you have no argument for the blabbermouth accusation."

"He does like to talk." Eve smiled, then her expression changed slightly. "You need to know, one way or another, about the marriage thing. I don't see any way around it. Travis is the logical next step." She took a long sip of her decaf. "So, what are you going to do this time? Keep Grant or send him packing?"

That was the million-dollar question...

Eve eyed the case of baked goods. "This morning has been far too exciting. I need a chocolate cupcake, stat."

CHAPTER 12

Grant slept late, but then it had taken him forever to fall asleep. He still felt like an asshole. At the same time...

Yellow dress. Lies. And *still* no other memories.

His wife would have answers to all his questions, wouldn't she? Where was his family? Did he have one? Besides her, of course. Where had he grown up? Did he have a job?

Were they still married?

He should've just confronted her straight on, no games. He'd let his frustration get the best of him; as if that was an excuse. He should've confronted her in a different way, he should've been honest. One of them should be. But he hadn't been thinking clearly; hell, he hadn't thought at all, he'd let his anger lead the way.

Of all the questions he wanted to ask Ivy, the one he wanted an answer to most desperately was... why? Why the lies? Why leave him in the dark when she had all the answers? Last night had left him frustrated and feeling as if this one part of his life, the one he could hang onto, was unfinished. Like everything else.

It was close to noon when he left Ivy's house. The front door hadn't been locked, so he left it that way, just closed it behind him and started walking. Maybe Mystic Springs was one of those towns where people didn't always lock their doors. Like Mayberry.

Why did he remember Mayberry so easily but still recalled next to nothing personal about himself? Nothing beyond a wedding.

He was supposed to be working for Ivy, sweeping floors or washing dishes, but he was in no hurry to get started. Walking was good for him, so he decided to make a loop through town. He passed several interesting looking shops but didn't stop at any. Maybe if he found he had money, somewhere, anywhere, he'd support the town's economy. Until then...

At the end of the row of businesses, he turned and saw an unfinished mural painted on what had once been a plain concrete block wall. Just a few days ago it had been gray and unadorned, he was sure of it. The colors were so vivid, they caught his eye. The scene was Mystic Springs at night, as near as he could tell, with stars in the sky and a good portion of the shopping district laid out below. The Egg was located at one far end; woods at the other. It was a fair representation, though the colors were brighter than real life and everything was not to scale. Still, he'd call it art.

He crossed the street and turned back toward the bakery. Might as well get this over with. Would Ivy put him to work or kick him out? He was pretty sure that woman could put any man on his ass, if she put her mind to it.

His wife. Ex-wife? Estranged wife? First wife? Somehow he had to find out.

Travis Benedict was coming out of his office as Grant walked by. The smile the police chief cast his way was... weird. Off, somehow. Normally the guy was an open book, or seemed to be. Could he trust even that impression? At the moment, everyone and everything was suspect.

"Good afternoon," Benedict said as he fell into step beside Grant.

"Is it?"

"Someone's in a bad mood."

"You get shot and see what it does for your mood."

"Now, now, all in all you've done pretty well for yourself. You got off to a shaky start, but you're healing well, you're getting around great, I've found no warrants for your arrest, you're shacking up with my sister-in-law…"

"And I remember nothing." *Almost* nothing. "I wouldn't call sleeping in Ivy's guest room shacking up."

"Whatever," Travis said in an offhand manner. "You know, it's really time you started getting some memories back."

"Past time," Grant mumbled.

Travis slipped past him and opened the door to Eve's Cafe. Several tables and booths were taken, but the place wasn't packed. "Let me buy you lunch."

Since he wasn't quite ready to face Ivy…

"Sure. Why not?"

Something smelled great. So far he'd been eating at The Egg and the B&B, and he'd had soup at Ivy's house. None of it had been terrible, but nothing had tasted the way the food in this cafe smelled.

Travis took him to the counter, where they claimed a couple of stools. He ordered the special for both of them. Might've been nice to look at a menu, but if that smell was the special he'd take it.

While they waited, the police chief tried to strike up a conversation.

"Remembering anything at all?" he asked.

Should he tell about the memory of marrying Ivy? Did Travis already know? If he did, and it was a secret, why? None of it made any sense. "No. Finding me a wanted man anywhere?"

"Nope. Not yet, anyway. I still have Interpol on standby."

Apparently that was a joke. Grant didn't feel much like kidding around at the moment. "I'm guessing you still have no idea who shot me."

"Not a clue."

"Since it's been a week and no one's come after me yet, I'm going to assume whoever shot me isn't a motivated hit man."

"Probably not."

"So maybe this afternoon you can get me the hell out of this damned town."

Travis looked surprised, for half a second. "Where do you want to go?"

That wasn't a no...

"I don't care. Anywhere but here will do." Maybe he had married Ivy, once upon a time, but somehow, some way, it had ended, and she'd rather lie about it than tell him the truth. Whatever the reason for secrecy, she preferred lies. Why should he stay?

Before they could make plans for escape, a pretty waitress with short dark hair placed two identical plates before them. Chicken casserole. While he had limited memories, he was pretty sure chicken casserole was right up there with cabbage, in his list of preferred foods.

But Travis was buying, his wife ran the place, so maybe he knew what he was doing.

Grant took a bite of the casserole. It was good. Really tasty. He immediately wanted more so he shoveled in a couple more bites, eating too fast. He'd had maybe half a dozen forkfuls down when it started.

He wasn't sure what to call the sensations, not really. They were foreign to him, unknown, not memories exactly, but intense recollections of sensations, emotions. Exhilaration. Heartbreak. Pain. Love. Hate. Confusion. Lots and lots of confusion.

Then there was that memory of marrying Ivy. Ivy in a yellow dress. Smiling. Loving him as much as he loved her. From there it grew, the memories coming fast and furious, almost too much to take.

Baseball, disappointment and success, thrill and pain.

Ivy, Mystic Springs, thinking he'd found a home here. The wedding had been real, but he remembered now that it had just been for show. No, not for show. It had been just for *them*, but it wasn't legal. It had never been legal.

She'd done something to him, though he didn't entirely understand what. With tears in her eyes she'd given him something to drink. Since he'd loved and trusted her, when she said drink he did as he was told.

When he'd drunk whatever concoction she'd given him, his memories of her and this place had disappeared. He'd forgotten her for a long time. Years! And now, out of nowhere, the memories were all back.

Family. He had parents, two brothers, a sister-in-law, and a nephew. They weren't especially close, but neither were they estranged. Why weren't they looking for him?

Because he'd told them he needed some time alone, he remembered in a flash, and they were giving him the space and time he'd said he needed.

He'd decided to do some camping, fishing, boating. Alone. He'd thought nature would soothe him. Why had he chosen this part of Alabama for his getaway? Of all the places in the world, why here? Maybe somewhere in the back of his mind he'd remembered Ivy and that had guided him here.

Getting shot…

He'd been fishing, and it had just happened. There was no face, no name. He could remember falling into the water and being washed away, and then…

Mystic Springs, again.

It was the food, he knew that now. Five years ago Ivy had warned him that her twin's creations could spark memories and emotions, and it was especially strong in newcomers. When he'd been here before, Ivy had done all the cooking in those small rooms over the bakery. He'd never understood what she'd said about the cafe. There had been other weird things she'd told him about the town, but none of it had made sense. And he hadn't cared. He'd only cared about her.

In that room over the bakery they'd made love, fallen head over heels, and made plans she'd stolen away.

He instinctively picked up his plate and tossed it to the wall behind the counter, barely missing the waitress who'd delivered the cursed food. She ducked, shouted "Fuck!" as she rolled away. Grant didn't stop there. His water glass followed. The plate of rolls. A bottle of ketchup that spun end over end until it hit a wall. It would've been satisfying if it had exploded, but it didn't. Damn plastic bottle just bounced off the wall and dropped to the ground.

Benedict tried to stop him, but Grant barely heard the man who attempted to talk reason. Reason? There was none.

Grant turned on the police chief. "You've known all along who I am. So does your wife, and Ivy, and half the people in this room. What the hell! In the past week not one of you could've filled me in on the secret? Not one of you could've helped me?"

He didn't need them. All he had to do now was call someone to come get him. One of his brothers. Ken lived closer than Billy, but was still hours away. Maybe a friend. He actually had friends, good friends who'd be glad to help him out.

He had money. He didn't need to take charity guest rooms and buy used t-shirts. By God, he had the means to take care of himself.

Grant took a moment to look around. He'd made a real mess. He looked at the waitress—Ruby, her name tag read—and said, "I'll pay for the damage."

"How about grab a mop and help me clean up this mess!" she snapped.

"I won't be here that long." He turned to tell Benedict to shove it, but the police chief had disappeared. Just as well. Grant didn't have anything good to say to the man.

~

It had been a busy enough day, but the stream of customers that were in and out of the bakery did nothing to distract Ivy. Every time the door opened, she expected to see Grant come walking in. If she was smart, she'd tell him to get out of her house and out of town, but she'd never been smart where Grant was concerned.

She was thinking of closing up early and hunting her house-guest down, just to get it over with, when Travis poked his head in.

"We could use your help next door."

"I've told Eve a hundred times, I don't care how busy she gets I'm not waiting tables."

"It's Grant."

Ivy froze. What the hell was Grant doing at Eve's? Everyone in town should've known that putting a plate of Eve's memory-inducing food in front of Grant would be a bad idea. One look at Travis's guilty face, and she knew who'd done it. What the hell was he thinking?

"Okay, yeah, it was a bad plan that went over even worse than I thought it would."

Ivy took off at a run without even bothering to take off her lavender apron. What did Grant remember? Everything? Bits and pieces? One thing for sure, there was no reason for him to stay here. He had options, options they'd done their damnedest to keep from him.

Travis followed her. Grant had left the cafe and was stalking down the sidewalk. Toward her house? The doctor's office? Where would he go, and what would he do?

"Grant!" she called, breaking into a run.

He turned and looked at her. Oh, he was so angry, her first

instinct was to turn around, go back to the bakery, and lock the door.

And hide, the way she'd been hiding for the past five years.

"Have you come to stop me, pretend wife?" he asked.

Travis mumbled something, but Ivy wasn't paying attention to him. At all.

"We have a lot to talk about."

"We have nothing to talk about," Grant said. "I see it all now." He took a step closer. "I started to remember days ago, and you know it. I told you. Then yesterday I saw that damned yellow dress hanging in your closet, and a few more pieces fell into place. I loved you. I thought you loved me, but you… you poisoned me to make me forget. How the hell did you manage that?"

The dress! How could she have been so stupid?

How could she have realized he'd remember that dress, or anything at all of her?

"I wanted you to have everything you wanted, and that…"

He took another step closer. "I wanted *you*! More than baseball, more than money, more than anything. I wanted you."

"You said that, but…"

"I meant it."

Had he? Had the pain of the past five years been unnecessary? She'd never know. There was no way to know.

"Well, the wedding wasn't real. We did it just for us, on a whim." She tried to force her tone to be light, carefree. It didn't quite work.

"I remember," he said, his voice low and dark.

Travis muttered something again.

"So there's nothing holding you here," she said. "Travis was wrong when he said you needed to stay. He's wrong a lot."

She glanced over her shoulder to glare at her brother-in-law. "Why are you still here?"

"Because I'm not done."

"You are most definitely done. Scoot." She fluttered her fingers in his direction and faced Grant again. "We wanted to know who shot you and why, but it's been more than a week and Travis has nothing. Maybe you'd be better off elsewhere. It's not like we're actually married." She tried to laugh, but it didn't work.

Travis stepped around them and inserted himself into the middle of the conversation. Literally. He held up his hand, one palm toward her, the other toward Grant. "Before we do anything, we need to talk."

"Haven't we talked enough?" Grant snapped.

"Apparently not," Travis said. "After I talked to Eve this morning, I did a little checking online. Maybe you two didn't file the marriage certificate with the county." He looked to Grant and then back to Ivy. "But someone did."

CHAPTER 13

He was married. To Ivy.

The doc had told him his memories might come back slowly or all at once. He hadn't warned him that having them all come back in a flood would be so overwhelming. There was too much to take in; too much to process.

"Why didn't you tell me?" he asked.

"What was the point?" Ivy appeared to be overwhelmed herself. She'd truly believed the wedding had been a farce. A bit of fun, maybe.

Grant tried to grasp what had been in his head at the time. It was there, a part of the flood of information. He'd been crazy about her, that much was clear. Getting married when they'd only known one another for a month or so had been an insane idea, but one they couldn't shake. What was the solution? Say the words, make it as real as possible without bothering with the legalities. Ivy had never expected to find herself legally a wife. *His* wife.

"Does the truth need to have a point?" he snapped. "For the past week you let me flounder around like a fish out of water, wondering who I was and how I got here. You let me care about you with that lie between us." Care about? He'd loved her, then and now. He didn't dare say that out loud.

"I didn't tell you because you can't stay," Ivy said. Were those tears in her eyes? No, not tears. Not for Ivy. Something in the air, he supposed. "This isn't your world. You *can't stay*. What's the point of this conversation?" she snapped. "We can't go back, I can't undo what's been done."

One of the memories that had blindsided him in the cafe came back, more slowly this time. And still, it didn't make sense. "You gave me something, and then you cried." She did cry; she did feel sorrow. Regret? "After that... why didn't I remember you all these years? Why didn't I even wonder why I had a missing chunk of time? Somehow you erased this place, and yourself, and the wedding that you thought didn't count. How..."

Odd things had happened last time he'd been here. Little memories trickled in. At first Ivy had tried to brush off the weird things he'd seen, but eventually she'd told him the truth about Mystic Springs. At the time they'd believed he'd stay, and if he was going to stay, she said, he had to know the truth. He hadn't believed her at first, but she'd convinced him.

"You poisoned me," he whispered.

"I did not!" She looked sheepish. "It was amnesia punch, administered to erase what you knew so you could..."

"So I could what?" he snapped when she faltered.

"So you could have what you wanted! So your dreams could come true!" She looked and sounded as frustrated as he felt. "I wanted us to have a life together, but having what I wanted would've meant robbing you of what *you* wanted."

He moved a step closer. "I wanted you more!"

Ivy looked as if he'd slapped her. She was stunned. Horrified. Surprised.

Grant said the words again, without so much heat. "I wanted you more."

He looked over Ivy's shoulder to the police chief, who stood behind her. Benedict had gone pale; he wanted to escape, but maybe he felt that walking away at this moment would be seen as cowardly. Grant felt more than a little cowardly himself. Escape seemed like a fine idea.

"Get me out of here. Eufaula, I guess. I need to make a few phone calls, see a real goddamn doctor, and file a police report with a real goddamn police officer."

"Hey," Travis said softly, then he shrugged his shoulders in resignation.

Grant looked at Ivy. She didn't move closer. She didn't say a word, not to encourage him to stay or to leave. "Maybe I was just a bit of fun for you, a summer fling, but I did love you, more than anything. Don't worry. I'll file for divorce as soon as I get out of this damned town."

"You never used to curse so much," she said.

"I never had much reason, until now." He turned his back on Ivy because he couldn't bear to look at her for another minute. He was so angry he trembled deep down.

Benedict joined him, matched his stride, and he walked toward the police car that was parked in front of the station. "Do you know who shot me?" Grant asked.

"No," Benedict said.

"Why should I believe you?"

Travis hesitated, then said, "I guess I wouldn't blame you if you didn't."

Grant opened the passenger door and sat, ready to get out of town, ready to leave all this behind him. Travis snagged car keys from his pocket, then got behind the wheel and turned to face him.

"You really should have another dose of punch before we..."

"No," Grant snapped. "I won't tell anyone what's going on here." He glared at Benedict. "Who'd believe me if I did? It's... insane."

"It is that." Travis slammed the key into the ignition and turned.

Nothing happened.

He tried again, and again… nothing.

"Dead battery?" Grant asked, but even as the words left his mouth he had second thoughts.

"One way to find out." Travis left the vehicle and headed down the sidewalk. He stuck his head into a dress shop, said something Grant couldn't hear, and came out with another set of keys in his hand. He got behind the wheel of a red compact car, which started on the first try.

With a sigh of relief, Grant got into the passenger seat.

As he closed the car door, the engine died. When Travis tried again to start the engine, it was dead.

Travis looked at Grant and raised his eyebrows. "Looks like you're not going anywhere just yet. Someone wants you to stay put."

"That's ridiculous," Grant said, but in the back of his mind he knew Travis was telling the truth.

Like it or not, he was trapped in Mystic Springs.

~

I loved you. Past tense.

I wanted you more.

Ivy ran back to her bakery, closed and locked the door, and hunkered down behind the glass case that was filled with glorious baked goods.

She shook to her bones.

She was, and had always been, a confident woman. Second guessing was not in her nature. She'd been so certain she was doing the right thing when she'd sent Grant away. It had been for his own good. Leaving was what he needed, what he wanted whether he knew it or not!

And yet... she'd regretted that decision every day since. She'd never recovered, never moved on.

She'd loved Grant, too. She loved him still.

She only had a few minutes to wallow before someone started knocking on the door. Ignoring the knock didn't help. It kept on and on and on. Whoever was there wasn't going away.

After a couple of long minutes she stood and shouted, "Go away!" Only then did she notice it was Grant pounding on the glass door. Travis was right behind him. "You're supposed to be gone!"

Grant just glared at her.

Gathering her composure as best she could, Ivy headed for the door, unlocking it and opening it wide.

"What have you done?" Grant asked.

"Nothing!"

Travis stepped around Grant and placed himself between them. Chief Benedict; peacemaker. "Are you sure? Maybe it's unintentional, maybe you don't realize you're doing it."

"I'm confused," Ivy whispered.

"Someone, or something, doesn't want Grant to leave. My car wouldn't start."

Ivy rolled her eyes. "Seriously? Try another vehicle!"

"We tried four," Grant said. "As soon as I'm in the car, it goes dead."

"I bake," Ivy said. "The flavors are accentuated and there are no calories, but that's it. I don't have the kind of power it would take to strand anyone anywhere. Besides, I want him to go. It's... for the best. For everyone." Maybe if she said that often enough, she'd start to believe it.

"Your Granny Pearl was a powerful witch, and your dad was no slacker. Maybe the Franklin magic didn't skip you, maybe it's just been sleeping."

"I don't want Grant to stay!"

"Maybe subconsciously..." Travis began.

"No!"

"Who else would want him to stick around that badly?"

She didn't have an answer to that question.

Travis backed toward the door. "If nothing else, you two need to talk. Privately. Maybe once you work out your issues, whatever's holding Grant here will resolve itself."

The last thing she wanted was to be alone with her… shit, with her *husband*. "I guess we can give it a try," she said in a low voice.

Grant pointed a finger at her. "No fucking amnesia punch. Give me your word."

"Fine."

"Say it," Grant insisted as Travis left the bakery.

"No amnesia punch this time." She took a deep breath and let it out slowly. "You have my word."

CHAPTER 14

Ivy locked the door and turned off the purple *Open* sign. She looked about as excited to be alone with him as he was to be stuck here with her.

She'd lied.

She'd poisoned him with her damned punch, she'd robbed him of his memories. His memories of her.

Grant was furious with Ivy, but he still loved her. Even though he hadn't remembered her, he'd always loved her. He knew that now. He understood why no woman had ever been quite right for him, and why he'd always had a thing for redheads.

Escape had seemed like a good idea a few minutes ago, but at the moment his initial instinct to leave town struck him more like running away from his problems than getting to a place where he might be able to fix them. Did he do that, did he run? Looking back… maybe. That's what he'd been doing when he'd landed here, five years ago. That's what he'd been doing this time, too, with his career on hold, his future uncertain.

Ivy brushed past without looking at him. "We can talk upstairs," she said. "If someone comes by and sees us, they'll just keep knocking until I let them in or tell them to fuck off. That's sometimes tempting, but it's not good for business."

"Are you doing this?" he asked as he followed her into the kitchen, which was all stainless steel and sparkling white tile. "Have you trapped me here?"

"No," she snapped, then she turned to look at him. "I don't think so," she added in a lower voice. "What goes on in this town is never quite as simple as it seems. You'd think it would be, but a magical life is no less messy than a normal life. Things don't always work as they should. The answers are never as clear as we'd like them to be."

Shot and stranded. And he'd thought being up for contract without any offers coming in was bad...

"Do you know who shot me?"

"No," she said with such conviction he believed her. "If I did... I don't know if I'd kill them or thank them. They hurt you, but they also brought you back to me. Even if it wasn't for very long, I'm... I'm glad."

Oddly enough, so was he.

She didn't linger in the kitchen but continued to a back stairwell that led to a couple of rooms over the bakery. Ivy had lived there, once upon a time. He'd lived there with her, for a few weeks. He followed her up the narrow staircase to the room where they'd spent their honeymoon. New memories assaulted him. Maybe they hadn't gone on a fancy vacation, but their honeymoon had been fine...

What had once been a bedroom was now an office, but the main room, which was a living room and kitchenette combined, still had a couch and a couple of chairs. They'd had sex on that couch, more than once. And in that big chair, and...

"Maybe we should find another place to talk," he said. The memories he'd just recovered were still too raw. For Ivy maybe they'd faded over time, but for him everything was new and real.

The love, the heat, the hurt. He felt it all as if they'd made love on that couch just yesterday.

"You don't want to walk out that door, not just yet," Ivy said, going to the front window and looking down on the street.

"Why not?"

She turned to face him, after pulling the heavy curtains shut. "Mystic Springs has a fully functioning gossip line. By now everyone will know what happened next door. Some of them will know that we're actually…" She swallowed, looked away before finishing with a whispered, "…married. A few more will have heard that for one reason or another you're trapped here. Even if you can't see them on the street, they're there, watching and waiting." She caught his eye. "You might love the limelight, but I've always hated making a spectacle of myself."

"So, how long will we be trapped here before you feel like facing the music?"

"You're angry."

"You bet your ass I am."

She walked to the counter and got coffee out of a cabinet by the old fridge.

"I don't want any damned coffee," he said.

"I do," she countered. "If I go downstairs for what's already made, you can bet someone will be looking through the front window."

He watched her for a moment as she went through the motions. Coffee and filters, water, that old coffee maker, matching cups from the cabinet…

"You're hiding," he whispered.

"What?" She turned and leaned against the counter while the coffee maker sputtered and dripped. Well, dribbled.

"You hide," he said. "You always have. We're a pair, aren't we? I run away. You hide." A realization struck him, hard. "It's why you've never left this town, why you sent me away. You're afraid."

"I'm not afraid of anything!"

"You're afraid of everything." He walked toward her. "Life. Love. Stepping outside this neat little world you've made for yourself."

"I haven't made a world and let's be honest, life in Mystic Springs is anything but neat. But I was born into it and I do the best I can with what I've been given."

"We all make our own world. We fill it with love or hate, with happiness or misery. Sure, bad things happen, and good things happen, but in between there's just life." He reached out and touched her face. "We had something special, and you threw it away because it scared you."

"I threw it away for you," she argued.

"If that was true, you would've given me a choice in the matter."

"You would've chosen me," she whispered.

"I would have."

"Eventually you would've resented me for robbing you of your dream."

"The choice would've been mine."

She was trapped between him and the counter. The coffee maker sputtered. He was close enough to feel her tremble and her heat, to smell her. She smelled of cinnamon and sugar, and now that his memories had returned with a vengeance, he remembered how much he'd loved the way she smelled.

Her smile. Her rare laugh. The way she turned her head; the way she looked at him.

He leaned in slowly and kissed her. She kissed him back, melted into him, and wrapped her arms around his waist.

A lot of their history and their present was complicated. Messy. Uncertain. But when it came to this… they'd always done this part right, hadn't they? Last night they'd set things into motion, but anger and lies had come between them. There were no more lies. At the moment, the anger he'd experienced was gone, fading away to be replaced with more complicated emotions.

"I want you," he said, resting his head on her shoulder and pulling her close.

Ivy sighed. "I want you, too." She raked a hand through his hair. "I've tried to seduce you more than once, but so far I've been a failure."

He backed away a little. "Try again."

From the moment she'd first seen Grant, more than five years ago, she'd believed he was meant to be hers. The sex had been out of this world; they'd stayed awake all night, just talking. Well, not *just* talking, but there had been plenty of conversation among other things. And then she'd robbed him of the big choice. Her or baseball.

She'd robbed herself, too; she knew that now.

She should've left the bed here, instead of moving it out to make herself an office. Too late for that. No bed, but the couch was long and wide. It would do.

Ivy removed her apron and tossed it aside. She kicked off her sneakers and pulled her shirt over her head. Before she removed her bra and jeans, she reached out to help Grant. She went right for the button on his jeans. He answered by reaching around and unsnapping her bra. She pressed her hand to his erection, already imagining what was to come. She went up on her toes and kissed him, deeply, completely, while she stroked.

Okay, this wasn't seduction, exactly. But since when had *subtle* been her style? Never.

They were both naked before she laid down on the couch. Grant was there in a heartbeat, kissing her deeply as they both set aside everything that had gone wrong. Her mistakes; his bad fortune. Was getting shot such a bad thing if it brought him back to her?

This they could do right. Skin to skin was the most exquisite sensation she'd ever known. It soothed and aroused her at the same time, it took her to another place, to another world. This wasn't her world or his, it was theirs. The magic they created was as real as any other.

Grant slipped a hand between their bodies and touched her, caressed her where she was already wet and craving him. How had she lived without him all these years? How had she managed to survive? She wasn't going to allow him to make her come and then walk away, as he had last night.

She wrapped her legs around his hips and then he was inside her. A cry escaped her lips. This was heaven. She closed her eyes and savored, but the savoring didn't last long. Her body demanded more, it demanded what she'd craved for the past five years. The connection, the blending of his body and hers, the pleasure that drove her to take more, and more.

Years had passed; they weren't kids anymore, weren't the same people, but this was in many ways the same. Neither of them were living in the past, not at this moment. They were here, they were together, and nothing else mattered. Nothing but the end he drove her to.

She cried out, as wave after wave wracked her. Ribbons of pleasure brought tears to her eyes. Grant came with her, filled her one more time and shook.

For a long moment they didn't move. They held onto one another, breathed deeply, clung to each other on the too-narrow couch.

"You're far too easy to seduce," she whispered.

"I'll play hard to get next time."

She laughed a little. "I don't think so."

Grant raised his head and looked down at her, and the last of her laughter died. Oh, those eyes. The way he looked at her. The love in those eyes. At the moment, his love was tinged with anger. Would he ever forgive her? Was forgiveness too much to ask for?

"What now?" he asked.

"We can stay here until the excitement dies down," she said. "We won't starve, if you don't mind eating cupcakes and cookies for every meal, and there's plenty of coffee."

"How long do you think that will take?" he asked.

She sighed. "It might be a while. The town hasn't seen this much excitement in, well, months. We take our entertainment wherever we can find it."

"We're entertainment for your friends and neighbors."

"Absolutely."

Grant brushed a strand of hair away from her face. "I want you in a real bed, and I want everyone in town to know that you're my wife."

"I thought you were eager to get out of town, to leave me and all of this behind. Why the sudden change?"

"The fact that we're both naked might have something to do with it."

Their state of undress certainly affected her mood. "Everyone will be watching..."

"Let them watch," Grant whispered, and then he kissed her again. "I'll protect you. If you feel like you're making a spectacle of yourself, lean into me. Hide in me, Ivy." He was hard again; she was ready. A shift of her body and a wiggle of her hips, and he was inside her.

She moved more slowly this time, was not so frantic in her motions or her drive. But she *was* driven, and so was he. The rest of the world melted away until there was only the two of them and the passion they shared.

And in that moment, Ivy found and cherished the happiness that had eluded her for the past five plus years.

CHAPTER 15

Ivy had insisted on waiting until dark to leave the bakery for their walk home, even though Grant had tried his best to convince her that making a spectacle of herself wasn't always a bad idea. The sky was still gray, so it wasn't as dark as she would've liked it to be when they walked out of the bakery and she locked the door behind them. Most businesses would be closed, she conceded; traffic should be light.

He had to admit, she hadn't been exaggerating about the interest they were sure to rouse. In his week in town, he hadn't seen this many people on Main Street. They loitered in front of businesses that were done for the day. As he and Ivy walked down the sidewalk toward the residential section of town, he saw people down the side streets; on their own sidewalks or in yards, alone or with neighbors. He'd been ogled plenty in his time as a baseball player, and this felt much the same.

Grant smiled and waved at several of those who stared in the most audacious manner. Most of them looked away quickly; others smiled sheepishly and offered a return wave.

He refused to feel guilty about walking down the street with his wife.

His wife. That was going to take some getting used to. There were still so many questions to be answered. Not only did they not know who'd shot him, there was the mystery of who'd filed the paperwork that made their impromptu wedding legal. The preacher? His wife? Who else could've done it?

He remembered signing the papers the preacher had pushed at them. He didn't remember what had happened to the paperwork after that. Those mundane details hadn't been important; they'd been easily dismissed. He'd been giddy, and so had Ivy. The fact that the wedding was secret, a moment just for them, only aroused them more. And that was saying something.

He'd wanted Ivy to be his wife more than he'd wanted anything before or since.

The wedding had happened not long before the phone call that had changed everything, but had Ivy somehow known that he wasn't going to stay? Was that why they'd had what they'd believed to be a fake wedding?

Had she known all along it wouldn't last?

On the street where Ivy lived, it seemed every single neighbor was sitting on their front porch. They all smiled and waved. Ivy ignored most of them, but she did wave—reluctantly—at Travis and Eve, just before she opened her own front door and slipped inside.

Once they were safely indoors she leaned against the entryway wall, closed her eyes, and sighed.

"See? That wasn't so bad," he said gently.

Her eyes popped open. "Not so bad? Half the town watched us walk from the bakery to this house!"

"So?" He took her in his arms. "Let 'em look, let 'em stare to their heart's content. I don't know what's going to happen next. No one does. But tonight you're my wife and I don't care who knows it."

"But..."

"One day at a time, Ivy. One day..."

The knock that interrupted his words was soft, almost too soft. Ivy stilled, as if she was planning to freeze in place until the intruder went away. As if everyone in town didn't know exactly where they were.

Grant turned around and opened the door himself, since it looked like Ivy was going to ignore the knock entirely. He wasn't surprised to see Travis and Eve standing there.

Eve looked so much like Ivy, but at the same time he noted the subtle differences everyone else seemed to miss. The eyes were a slightly different color. Eve's were a bit more green; Ivy's a tad more blue. There was a slight rounding to Eve's cheeks, maybe because she was expecting a baby, or so he'd heard. Their hair, in color and style, was almost identical.

Almost.

Ivy's twin carried a covered casserole dish in her hands.

Grant held out one hand, palm forward. "Thanks, but no thanks." He had no desire to be flooded with memories and emotions again thanks to some kind of freaky chef voodoo. Once had been enough.

Eve walked inside, skirting around Grant. "It's unlikely you'd be affected again, especially so soon, but I had one of the new girls make this dish just in case. She needs the practice, and I need to know if she can get the recipe right."

Grant backed up, and Travis entered the house behind his wife.

Not what he'd intended when he'd walked Ivy home. He'd be able to get rid of these two eventually, he was sure, but it wouldn't be soon enough to suit him.

He and Ivy followed the guests to the kitchen. "Man cannot live by cupcakes alone," Eve said in a light voice. "Lasagna might be just the thing. Since Travis had news, I thought I'd come along and bring your supper."

In the kitchen, the sisters shared a meaningful glance. Grant could almost decipher that look. The sisters were easy to read, in many ways. Eve was concerned, worried for her twin. And then she wasn't.

"What news?" Grant asked, turning to the police chief.

"A couple of things. I called the preacher's wife this afternoon. She's close to ninety, but her memory is still pretty good. Her husband found the marriage license after you two left and decided you'd just forgotten in your..." He cleared his throat. "In your haste."

"She remembered us?" Ivy asked.

"Vividly," Travis answered.

"She said she'd never seen a bride and groom more in love," Eve said with a wan smile. And then she grimaced. "You didn't even tell me!"

"I would've, if..." Ivy began.

"We'll hash it all out later," Eve said. "This is going to require a longer discussion than we have time for now."

Ivy seemed relieved not to have that conversation then and there.

"I also heard from the Eufaula chief," Travis said. "A hunter found your campsite. Since your phone and wallet were in the camper and it was clear no one had been there for days, he reported it to the police."

A phone. A wallet! They were small things, but made him feel more... real.

"I'm going to pick them up in the morning," Travis said. "Don't take it personally, but I don't plan to ask you to ride along. We don't want a repeat of today's fiasco."

"Thanks," Grant said, reaching out to shake the chief's hand. He didn't mind not going to Eufaula. A few hours ago he'd been eager to escape, but right now he was content to stay put.

That done, Eve and Travis said their goodbyes, and Grant was alone with Ivy once more. He had a lot of decisions to make, important decisions that would affect the rest of his life.

But he didn't have to make them tonight.

~

It was well after dark before Levi felt safe enough to claim a spot to spy upon Ivy's house. With half the town watching, it was important to be careful. He could shield himself, but with so many prying eyes about it was best to be cautious. He couldn't be found out; it wasn't time for revelations. Levi sat on a rock near the back corner of Ivy's yard, sheltered by trees that hadn't yet lost their leaves and the privacy fence her neighbors to the east had erected.

As if there was any true privacy in Mystic Springs.

His theory that Ivy's fall had nothing to do with love had been proven right. If love was the trigger, they'd all be free. They were not. If—*when*—that happened, he'd feel it.

"They're fucking their brains out at the moment, you know," his partner in crime said as she sat beside him and leaned against his thigh.

Levi rested a hand on Ruby's head and ruffled her short hair. "I can almost feel it."

"Can you see it?" she asked.

"No," he admitted. He'd discovered many special gifts since coming to Mystic Springs, but he didn't see auras the way Ruby did.

She lifted a hand and gestured, her fingers fluttering. "All the colors of the rainbow are drifting through the windows and trickling through the roof. I swear, there are colors pouring through that I've never seen before."

"Sex can be powerful," he said. Since he'd tried so hard to get Ivy to look at him in a romantic way, he might be jealous. He had been, he admitted, but right now he wasn't. Everything was proceeding as planned. The higher the heights Ivy reached, the greater the fall would be. He didn't really care who took her there.

"Your potion did the trick," she said. "I've seen people who are new to town be affected by Eve's food before, but not like that. Whitlock went absolutely nutso after just a few bites."

"It was simply an enhancer, a little something special to get the ball rolling." Memories of the past, of love, were important to the scheme. There was no time for a hampered Grant and an undecided Ivy to dance around one another.

Ruby sighed. "I'm so impatient for this to be done." She didn't sound impatient, but he understood. "I have plans, you know." She'd told him all about them, many times. He didn't mind hearing them again, and she loved sharing. "When I can be myself away from this place, I'm going to head to Seattle. The asshat is going to have his throat ripped out. Then maybe I'll do the same to his new, pretty wife. No, her first, then him. I want him to watch."

He should feel some sympathy for the man who'd seduced a young Ruby and then used her in his drug ring, before dumping her and marrying some rich man's spoiled daughter. But he didn't. The man would get nothing more than he deserved.

From all he could discover in his research there weren't many women in the Milhouse clan; the few he knew of didn't have the ability to shift. Ruby, a distant cousin who'd always steered clear of the Mystic Springs Milhouses, was the exception. The only one he'd found, at least.

They'd been sleeping together for a couple of months, but he didn't love Ruby and she didn't love him. She was convenient, nothing more. A way to blow off steam, to enjoy a bit of release while they planned the extrication of this town and the magic in it. They'd been very secretive, since he'd been trying to get Ivy to fall in love with him. Without success.

But that didn't matter. Nothing mattered but Ivy's destruction.

"I won't mind seeing Ivy get what's coming to her," Ruby said. "She can be a real bitch, you know."

"Trust me, I know."

"Eve is nice enough," Ruby mused. "You'd think her twin would've gotten a few of the more agreeable Franklin personality traits."

Would he have second thoughts if Ivy was an overall nicer person? If she'd at the very least agreed to one date with him, just to be polite? Maybe the old Levi would've felt some guilt about destroying a nice person, but the new Levi had no doubts at all. The ends really did justify the means.

He didn't need to sit here and watch a seemingly quiet house. Neither did Ruby. But they stayed. Ruby enjoyed her light show, while Levi bathed in the power he felt emanating from the house and the people in it.

He'd never known what real power was before coming here. The very real possibility that he might never have discovered who and what he was, that was a real nightmare. All he had to do now was make the best of it and build a truly spectacular life. He couldn't do that if he was trapped in Mystic Springs.

Before they left their perch in Ivy's back yard, Levi closed his eyes, waved his hand, and created a shield around himself. No one in Mystic Springs, not even the most powerful psychic, would be able to penetrate that shield. They wouldn't see what he was thinking, what he was planning, what he was doing. He did the same for Ruby. Couldn't be too careful. He magnified the shield every two or three days, to be safe.

As they walked through one back yard and into another, taking a direct route, Ruby asked, "Want to come back to my place for a while?"

"Not tonight."

If she was disappointed, she didn't let it show. Ruby didn't pout. He liked that about her. "Tomorrow, maybe," she suggested. "It's been a week and I'm getting a powerful itch."

"Maybe," he said.

She looked at him then, and even in the dark he could see the flash of anger in her eyes. Rejection was a trigger for her. She didn't take it well. No, she didn't pout, but she was planning to rip out the throat of the last man who'd forsaken her.

"Tomorrow," he said, glad there wouldn't be another full moon for more than a couple of weeks. The last thing he needed was Ruby coming after *his* throat in a rage.

He did kiss her goodnight, and watched her walk onto her own front porch. Her rental house was one of the smallest in town, and goodness knows the previous resident hadn't put any time or money into renovations or even basic upkeep. The house was decent enough; better than anything she'd had before coming here, he imagined.

When she was inside with the door locked and he felt that she was in for the night, he turned around headed back in the direction they'd come from, cutting through yet another back yard. He'd needed Ruby to be in place for the night, just to make sure she didn't follow. The last thing he needed was for her to see him headed for the B&B.

The big white house was dark but the front door was unlocked, as it often was. Levi slipped inside. The front door didn't squeal, as it sometimes did. He tried not to make any noise as he crept toward Molly's bedroom. Through the main room, down a dark hallway. A touch of light slipped from under the door, spilled onto an uneven wooden floor.

With his hand on the doorknob and his heart beating too fast, he thought of the woman who was waiting for him, and he smiled.

He opened the door quickly, startling Molly. She was sitting up in bed, holding a paperback that looked to have been read many times before. Mystery. The bedside lamp illuminated her and the innocuous cover.

Molly set the book aside, sighed, and tossed back the covers. "Where the hell have you been?"

CHAPTER 16

“I’m doing great,” Grant argued as they left the bakery and Ivy locked the door behind them. “I’m healing, I have my memories back, so what do I need the doc for?”

“You have an appointment,” Ivy argued. “Might as well let Levi look you over and give you the official all clear.”

Grant had spent the morning making phone calls. His parents. A brother. His agent. She’d been listening while he made those calls. He told them all the same thing. He was okay. He’d be home soon. He was taking a little time to get his head on straight so he could think clearly about what came next.

He didn’t tell them he’d been shot, or that he was married. Both of those tidbits would take time to explain, and would best be delivered face to face. At least, that’s what he told her.

Last night had been wonderful. She’d forgotten how good they were together. No, she hadn’t forgotten, exactly, she’d buried the memories deep because they hurt too much. Whenever they rose up she did her best to push them back down, to bury them deep.

Grant’s memory had failed spectacularly thanks to amnesia punch, but hers had been the subject of self-destruction.

She wasn't sure what might come next, if Grant would stay or if he'd go, if he'd want to remain married to her or not. If the answers to those questions weren't to her liking, it would hurt all over again. It would devastate her to lose him a second time. There were no doubts in her mind about what she wanted.

She wanted him to stay; she wanted desperately to be his wife. Ivy could no longer pretend that anything else would do. Could she keep him this time? Were love and happiness meant for her?

There was only one way to find out. In order to discover what this love meant for her, she'd have to take a chance. She wasn't particularly good at taking chances…

Levi saw Grant right on time. Ivy stood, planning to go to the examining room with him as she had before, but the doc waved her off. They'd be a while, he said. He wanted to conduct a complete exam, to make sure all was well. She started to argue—of course she did, that was her way—but then Grant nodded in agreement, easing her worries with a smile and a wink. Ivy reclaimed her seat. She didn't fume, exactly, but she didn't like being left behind.

Not even for a few minutes.

Ivy hadn't been sitting very long when she thought of the mural at the end of the street. She'd never been good at twiddling her thumbs; maybe she wasn't exactly ADD, but she didn't like being idle. She'd been waiting a few short minutes when she jumped out of the chair, left the office, and walked to the end of the street and the concrete block wall there that had once been ugly and plain.

The mural wasn't yet completed, but there had been progress since she'd seen it last. The town was more complete, as were the woods to the east. The houses in the background had been crudely drawn, they were incomplete, but Main Street was taking shape. The colors were vivid, bright, almost alive.

Who'd been working on this, and why hadn't she heard anyone else talking about the mural? Maybe they had been and she'd missed it. It wasn't like she'd been particularly sociable lately.

Or ever.

She noticed something new, something she'd missed when she'd first rounded the corner and started to study the mural. There were a couple of people on the street, in this newest version. Was that her, standing between the bakery and the cafe? Could be Eve, she supposed. It was hard to tell in a crudely painted figure. The red hair gave it away; that figure represented one of the Franklin twins.

At the other end of the street, not far from The Egg, a man seemed to be running. Had to be Grant. The form was blurry, but no other man in town sported that spiky hair-style, which was exaggerated in the painting. If that was Grant, then the redhead was probably her. Weird. Why paint the two of them and no one else? Maybe other people would appear on the mural as the work progressed. She hoped so. She'd always hated being the center of attention.

When Redmon had insisted on a complete exam, he hadn't been kidding. The doc took blood and carried it to a lab down the hall where he got the tests started, and then he had Grant strip to his underwear so he could check him from head to toe. Redmon hemmed and hawed, and he tsked now and then. He poked and prodded, sometimes to the point of pain. All in the name of good health, supposedly.

The doc didn't seem surprised that Grant's memories had returned all at once.

Most of them, anyway. Grant still couldn't tell Redmon or anyone else who'd shot him. He'd been fishing, there had been pain, and he'd fallen into the water. Whoever had shot him, it hadn't been a face-to-face attack.

Pure luck had carried him to the Mystic Springs riverbank. Well, knowing what he did of this place, maybe "luck" wasn't the right word. It had been meant to be. He and Ivy were meant to be.

Married. He still couldn't quite wrap his head around that fact.

After checking the lab results, Redmon returned with a nasty looking syringe. When Grant balked at the long, sharp needle, the doc just smiled.

"I detected a bit of infection in your blood analysis. This antibiotic will knock it right out."

"A pill won't do the trick?" He'd suddenly remembered that he didn't like needles. At all.

"Nope." With that, Redmon tugged at the elastic waistband of Grant's boxers and jabbed him in the hip.

It was not a pleasant experience. Damn, was an antibiotic supposed to burn like that? Must be powerful stuff. Or else he was a big baby where shots were concerned.

Grant dressed and headed for the lobby where a woman sat with a little boy, maybe seven years old or so, who was wearing a makeshift bandage on one knee. Mama was annoyed. The little boy had been crying, evidenced by red eyes and a tear-streaked face, but had stopped and was busy asking his mother one question after another. No Ivy, though he assumed she hadn't gone far.

"I know who you are!" The boy said, jumping out of his seat and running forward. "Grant Whitlock! I play baseball, too, but not shortstop. I'm in the outfield because I'm a good catcher. Not a catcher catcher, but you know, I can catch a popup. Sometimes."

"Austin..." Mama hissed.

"It's ok," Grant said with a smile. Ivy had explained to him how the entire town had kept his identity a secret, for a while. He should be pissed, but how could he be angry when he had Ivy back in his life?

Talking to kids was a part of his job, or had been. He hated dealing with the adults who were too-adoring, too invested. Some of the fans took it too far. The children were another story. There was something about the light in their eyes, the joy, that reminded him of all the reasons he loved baseball.

"Does Mystic Springs have a team?" he asked.

"It does!" Austin said. "We don't have enough players, but a couple of new kids have moved to town so maybe next year we can have a real team. If you're still here you can come see us play! I'll be even better next year, I bet. Maybe I can be a good hitter next year, like I'm a good catcher." He grimaced. "I'm not a very good hitter."

"I hope I can see you play next year," Grant said. He spotted Ivy on the sidewalk, smiled and waved bye to the kid, and headed her way.

Kids were sometimes annoying, even if he did like them well enough. They were definitely time-consuming; they changed their parents lives forever. He'd seen it happen to other players more than once, as their entire view of the world changed. Grant hadn't given much thought to having kids of his own in the past few years, but then he'd forgotten Ivy. Having her in his life again was changing his view of the world.

He wanted her to have his babies, wanted them to make little Ivys and little Grants. The desire was a startling primal instinct he hadn't experienced before. Children, babies, that wasn't something they'd talked about, but his brief time with Austin made him wonder. Did Ivy want kids? It was a talk they needed to have, one of these days.

But not today.

She looked annoyed. He'd seen that expression on her face a lot during his first few days in Mystic Springs.

"What's going on?"

"Come look at this," she said, taking his arm and heading toward the old folks' home.

"Why are we going to The Egg?"

"We're not."

There wasn't much else on this end of the street. Ivy passed a chocolate shop—hmm, chocolate shop, he'd have to check it out—and turned a corner.

He'd noticed the mural once before. It was interesting, with bright colors and a decent depiction of Main Street.

Ivy pointed and shook one finger. "It changed."

As it was obviously a work in progress, that wasn't surprising. "Since when?"

"Since five minutes ago!" She stepped closer, looked up, pointed again. "There were two people on the street, and I think it was supposed to be you and me. You were down by The Egg, I was at the bakery. You were running..."

"Maybe you imagined it," he suggested.

She didn't like that idea at all. "I did not."

"This is Mystic Springs, after all," he said. "Anything is possible, right?"

"Yes, but..."

He took her in his arms and kissed her. She seemed to take comfort from the kiss; she calmed down considerably.

After a spectacular kiss that didn't last nearly long enough, he took his mouth from hers. He didn't let her go, though, he kept his arms around her and stared at her face, taking it all in. "When I was a kid, I used to wish for superpowers. I thought it would be really cool to read people's minds, to know what everyone around me was thinking. Then I got onto social media and decided that power wasn't all it was cracked up to be."

She laughed.

"Maybe someone made this magical mural so that anyone who looks at it sees themselves, somehow."

"You don't see us."

"I'm not a Springer."

"Maybe you're right," she said, as they returned to the sidewalk arm in arm.

As they walked back toward the bakery, Grant experienced a wave of dizziness. He wobbled a little; Ivy steadied him.

"Are you okay?" she asked, concerned.

"Redmon said I have some kind of blood infection. Maybe that made me dizzy. No worries, love. He gave me a shot."

Ivy stopped in the middle of the sidewalk. "What kind of shot?"

"Antibiotics. No big deal. He ran a blood test and..."

Ivy tightened her grip on his arm. "There's no lab in that tiny doctor's office! If he needs bloodwork it goes to a clinic in Eufaula."

The dizziness got worse. Much worse. The world started to close in, gray at the edges, then swirling blackness. The world swam, his legs betrayed him, and Grant dropped to his knees. "Well, shit."

CHAPTER 17

Levi took care of the clumsy kid as quickly as possible and ushered him and his mother out the door so quickly the stupid woman stumbled as she hit the sidewalk and he locked the door behind her.

It wouldn't take Grant and Ivy long to figure out what he'd done. He had a few minutes, no more. Soon everyone would know, but they wouldn't understand why in time to stop him.

Before midnight, the barriers above and around Mystic Springs would fall.

His powers had come to life gradually. During that first visit he'd noticed that he always seemed to know what the people around him were thinking. It had been weird, even before he began to hear their voices. As his grandmother had explained what this town really was, she'd shown him a few new tricks. With a little practice, she'd said, he could do anything.

But only as long as he was here, in this little podunk town. One traffic light? They didn't even have that.

It hadn't taken him long to figure out that in addition to reading minds, it was possible for him to nudge people to do what he wanted. Some of them, anyway; the weak-minded always obeyed. Hand me that plant. Give me your money. Love me.

Ivy wasn't weak-minded; she'd never cooperated. No matter how he'd tried, he couldn't get through to her. Couldn't read her mind, either, or know what she might do next. There were a few in town like her, tough nuts to crack, but most of those around him were easy enough to influence.

Molly was a real pushover, eager to believe anything he suggested, willing to do whatever he wanted her to do. Ruby, not so much, though she wasn't nearly as difficult to manage as Ivy had been. He just had to work a bit harder with her.

He and Ruby had worked together well, so far, and it wasn't like he didn't enjoy her company. But she was a ballbreaker, too tough and demanding for his tastes. Molly did whatever he asked of her, whether he asked aloud or pushed a little at her tiny brain. She was malleable, compliant. And as temporary as Ruby. They each played a part, for now, but when he left he wouldn't be taking either of them with him.

The healing aspect of his powers hadn't been made clear to him until he'd been living in Mystic Springs for a few weeks. A wave of his hand, a bit of concentration, and he could heal anything. Well, he'd had luck with superficial injuries, but with practice he should be able to heal anything. Cancer. A bad ticker. Debilitating diseases patients would pay a small fortune to have wiped away.

He hadn't let anyone know what he could do. What a pain that would be! Every sick bastard would show up at his door, wanting to be healed. For free. Levi Redmon didn't do anything for free. When he could escape from this place and take this power with him, he was going to be rich. He wasn't the kind of man to give away his gifts.

The barriers that kept him trapped here had to be eliminated.

Some Springers could apparently leave town and keep their powers for a few days, or even a few weeks. He'd tested that on himself, and had failed miserably. By the time he'd reached Eufaula he was ordinary again. His abilities faded quickly, once he moved past the town limits.

Levi left through a rarely used back door and skirted behind the downtown buildings to a side street. Cutting this way and that, he made his way to the little rental house where he'd been living for months. The rent was ridiculously cheap. Once he left Mystic Springs, he'd never have to live in a cheap place again.

Inside the house, he removed his white coat and tossed it aside. His home was simply furnished with pieces that had come with the house. He had no photographs, no favorite paintings or doodads or even books. Anyone with a brain who looked at his house would realize his stay here was temporary. There were no hallmarks of a real home. It might as well be a hotel room.

The polo shirt and khakis he'd been wearing all day went next, dropped to the floor as the coat had been. He'd gotten very good at hiding who he was, what he was, not only with clothing and boring smiles and inane words, but with yet another ability he possessed. He hid beneath a shield as strong and impenetrable as the one he was about to destroy. Otherwise someone in this town would've outed him by now.

A few were suspicious of him in a way they didn't quite grasp. The old folks were the worst. Some of them disliked him, but they didn't know why. After tonight, they'd know. They should thank him for what he was about to do, but he knew damn well most of them wouldn't.

Real change didn't come without sacrifice. This was war.

As he dressed in black jeans and a black t-shirt, and donned the talisman his grandmother had made for him, he felt the power within him grow.

The feeling that washed through him could only be called giddiness, though he was not what anyone would call a giddy person. He was going to have everything he'd ever wanted. Soon.

Tonight. He was going to have money, all the women he desired, fast cars, and fine houses.

Killing one expendable person and destroying the woman who stood in his way wasn't too high a price to pay.

~

The Egg was closer than her house, and while Levi had locked up his office and disappeared—not that she'd let him anywhere near Grant—there was at least one nurse and a trained orderly in the retirement village.

With Travis's help, Ivy got Grant into his old room on the second floor. Seconds after he fell into the bed, he was unconscious.

"It was Redmon," Ivy snapped. "He gave Grant some kind of poison, or potion, or… something."

"How is that possible?" Travis asked. "Why would he…"

"I don't know, but he did."

The nurse on duty, Jane Milhouse, a member of the clan who did not shift—as far as anyone knew—checked Grant's vitals and declared him stable. His temp and blood oxygen were normal, his BP a little low but in the normal range. There were no obvious problems beyond the fact that he was unconscious.

Ivy asked, "You're just here part time, right?"

Jane, who was tall and sturdy, and whose only visible Milhouse trait was her thick brown hair, nodded. "Three days a week." As always, the female Milhouses were preferable to the males. Somehow they remained more civilized. None of them howled.

"Why did you never check with Doctor Redmon about helping out there?" How many times had Levi told her he couldn't find anyone to help, but that one mostly incompetent nurse's aide?

"Oh, I did. I asked him when he first opened, but he said he couldn't afford to hire any help. I meant to ask again, after he'd been in business a while." She frowned. "But I never did. I kept forgetting. I'd head that way intending to stop by, but I'd get distracted by ice cream or candy or a blouse in a window."

Jane didn't look like the kind of woman to be easily distracted.

Travis left the room, determined to track down Levi and get some answers. Before Ivy could ask Jane more questions—and she had plenty of them—Felicity Adams burst into the bedroom. The young girl was pale, but not as pale as her friend Bria.

"This isn't right!" Felicity said with a big dose of teen indignation. "This isn't how it's supposed to happen!"

"We had it all wrong," Bria whispered.

They had Ivy's full attention. "Explain?"

"It's all in the book," Felicity said. "At least, I thought it was. '*At the fall of Ivy, when the stars align, the protections that isolate Mystic Springs from the rest of the world might finally disappear.*'" The teen gestured wildly. "You fell in love. Why didn't it work? Why is Grant dying?"

Ivy felt the blood drain from her face. Lightheaded, she reached for the bedpost. "What do you mean, *dying*?"

"I can see it," Bria said softly. "His life is slipping away. It's like rainbows that are bright near his body but they grow fainter as they drift away. He'll be dead by midnight."

"No." Ivy shook a finger at the two girls. "I won't allow it."

"There's an old woman here, and she told me so," Bria said. "I don't think she's happy about it. This wasn't the plan. He wasn't supposed to be this way."

"What old woman?" Ivy snapped. In her head the words *dead by midnight* danced and played, like a bright neon sign. She tried to dismiss it, but those words wouldn't go away.

"Levi's grandmother, she says. She's not happy, but she says… she says maybe we can save him."

Ivy had no interest in helping Levi, but maybe saving him would also save Grant. "How?"

"It's in the book," Felicity said in a small voice.

"What fucking book?"

Both girls made faces, but Ivy wasn't going to apologize for cursing, not now.

Helen Benedict appeared; her two friends, her partners in crime, were with her. "Come along, ladies," she said. "The bus is waiting out front."

"What bus?" Ivy said.

Helen smiled wanly. "Dear, you need a bus to take you to the library."

CHAPTER 18

She could've run to the library faster than this, but everyone else was getting in her way. Helen and her friends took their time climbing the steps and taking their seats. Felicity and Bria were quicker, but the two old men who wandered on at the last minute were slower than the old women. Why were they here? They smiled like this was a damn field trip. Vince and Tobias Harper were longtime Springers of moderate abilities. Getting them off the bus would take longer than waiting for them to take their seats so the vehicle could get moving.

The trip was a short one, and during the minutes it took to get from one end of town to the other, Ivy made her way to the front of the bus to make sure she exited first. No way was she getting stuck behind the senior citizens this time. As soon as the doors whooshed open she was off the bus, running around the big vehicle and into the library.

Marnie was at the front desk. She was surprised to see Ivy, then obviously concerned when she saw the expression on her friend's face.

Ivy stopped near the desk where her friend sat. Marnie stood slowly and asked, "What's wrong?"

Two teenage girls and Helen had led her to this point, but now that she was here Ivy didn't know where to go, what to do. She knew this library well, had spent many hours here as a child, and as an adult. She'd never run across any old books with predictions, prophecies in which she played a part.

The door behind her opened; Helen and her cronies moved inside at an incredibly slow pace. They looked concerned but not panicked, and they were moving as quickly as they were able. Ivy felt her heart begin to pound harder than before as she waited for them to join her; she could barely catch her breath. Did Grant's life depend on what she might find here?

Felicity and Bria brought up the rear. As the girls slipped around the elderly folks, Felicity mouthed an apology. They'd lagged behind on someone's command. Helen's? Ginger's or Ramona's? It didn't matter. They were here now.

She needed them all; she needed all the help she could get.

Ivy followed the teens down one long aisle and then another, to the far back corner of the library. There wasn't anything of interest back here. The wall was bare. A slightly damaged folding table had been placed along one wall. Every other inch of the library was well used, so why was this area so neglected? It even looked a little dusty, and she knew Marnie made an effort to keep the place spotless.

Which was a clue in itself, one Ivy had missed but these young and powerful girls had not.

Felicity and Bria moved so they were in front of Ivy, almost as if they were protecting her. They joined hands, then lifted their free hands in sync. The empty wall shimmered. The folding table seemed to melt, then shifted into a massive antique wooden desk Ivy had never seen before. The corner of the library swam; a bright light made Ivy close her eyes for a moment. As she opened them everything before her melted, and what had been a dusty, empty area shifted until there were two mid-sized bookcases made of the same wood as the desk. Old books, ancient tomes, filled those bookcases.

Marnie cursed, in surprise not anger.

Ramona tsked, and whispered proudly to her friends, "I should've known these two would find it. I thought we'd hidden it well enough."

Ivy spun around. "Why would you go to so much trouble to hide these books?"

It was Ginger who answered. "There's too much power here for the diminishing abilities of Springers to handle. Would you give a nuclear weapon to a toddler? No, you would not."

Ivy had so many questions, no idea where to start, and no time for chitchat. She pointed to the old ladies. "We will have a long talk about all this later."

Felicity fetched an old leather book, the one necessary to find answers for today's urgent questions, and opened it carefully. The pages were yellowed and some of them were brittle. Ivy's first question might be why her name was in a book so old, a book obviously written long before she was born. But there was magic involved, and she knew there would be no good answer to that question.

Felicity placed the book on the desk and carefully leafed through several fragile pages in the middle of the book, until she came to the page she was searching for. Ivy moved closer and read over the girl's shoulder. The script was elaborate, the ink was smudged here and there, but most of the words were readable.

At the fall of Ivy, when the stars align, the protections that isolate Mystic Springs from the rest of the world might finally disappear. It will be her choice, her power that frees two hundred years or more of trapped magic.

The outside world will never be the same.

. . .

"There's so much in here," Felicity said. "History, prediction, potions, spells. I can't believe it was lost for so long."

"It wasn't lost, young lady, it was hidden," Helen said with a bite in her voice. "Some things are not meant to be known. Some secrets aren't meant to be shared. Why, there's no telling what you might've found."

Felicity's chin lifted in defiance. "We found Ms. Daniels' potion recipe to isolate the town, right where she'd hidden it, but we got rid of that."

"You did what?" Ramona snapped.

"We burned it, so it's gone and it won't come back," Bria said to her great-grandmother. "We don't want to be trapped here. I love my home, I love my family, but Mystic Springs feels like a prison sometimes, and that potion would've made it a real prison."

Marnie asked, "When did you girls find this... this hidden part of the library? Why didn't you tell me? What the hell..."

Ivy lifted a hand to silence her friend. "One thing at a time. This has something to do with Levi poisoning Grant, and I need answers. Now."

"When we read about the fall of Ivy, we thought it might mean, you know, falling in love. That would be nice, right? You would be happy and the barrier would fall, and we could leave town for as long as we wanted and take our magic with us. No one gets hurt just because you fall in love."

Ginger moved forward, leaning on her new cane and muttering to herself with each step. "No one is so naive as a teenage girl, I imagine. You have it all wrong." She forced her way past Bria and glared down at the page in question. "Nitwits," she snapped. "The ink of the first word is smudged. That's not *at* the fall of Ivy, it's *in*. As in an autumn that's special to her, a season of the year when the world is her oyster, so to speak."

"So, she can choose for the barrier to drop, just... wish for it, or ask, or cast a spell?"

It was Helen who answered. "I'm afraid it's not going to be

that simple."

The dinner crowd hadn't moved in yet, but there were a few stragglers in the dining room. Most of them were eating pie, drinking coffee, visiting with neighbors. Since so many people had started moving back to town, the cafe's business had really increased. In the next few months, she'd have a lot of decisions to make. Did she want to continue to work full time? Did she want to work at all? She was a wife now, and in a matter of months she'd be a mother. This was a life she'd never expected to have, and she wanted to enjoy it to the fullest. She had good help and she could hire more, if she needed to. But did she want to continue to cook six days a week? Was her gift with food truly her life's purpose?

Eve had her hands full, preparing the chicken and dumplings for tonight's customers. Pies were made; she'd bought cake and rolls from Ivy.

She hadn't seen Ivy nearly often enough in the week and a half since Grant Whitlock had returned. Her feelings were complicated. She wanted her sister to be happy, to have love as she did. But Grant had broken Ivy's heart. Even if the break had been Ivy's choice, not his, he was still to blame.

Maybe that wasn't fair.

Travis came into the kitchen, as he often did this time of day. She'd tried to get him to wear a hairnet when he hung out in her domain, but he was having none of it.

As if it was possible to contaminate her food...

"What's going on at the library?" he asked.

"I don't know." There were no windows in the kitchen, which was located at the back of the cafe.

"The Egg bus is there. Don't they usually go to the library on Monday?"

It didn't bother her, but Travis could be a stickler for routine.

"Someone needed a book," she said. "A bus full of old people hardly calls for a visit from the cops," she teased.

He walked to her, kissed her lightly, and said, "I'm going to check it out anyway. Back in a few."

She watched him walk away; the idea of spending more time with him and less in the cafe seemed very appealing. He really needed to hire a couple of people, too. A deputy, maybe two. If Mystic Springs kept growing, he was going to need help. Besides, when the baby arrived she wanted him home more. Was that too much to ask?

A few minutes later, Ruby came into the kitchen. That girl had been a godsend! If anyone could handle this place in Eve's absence, it was her.

"What can I do?" Ruby asked.

"Nothing," Eve responded. "Sit down and have a big glass of water. Everyone loves chicken and dumplings night. You'll be plenty busy once customers arrive."

Ruby smiled, but she didn't sit or head back to the main room for water. She walked straight to Eve, drew a hand from behind her back, and with one quick move stabbed Eve in the neck with a long needle.

It hurt, then whatever Ruby sent into Eve's bloodstream *burned*.

"Sorry," Ruby whispered as she caught a slumping Eve in her strong arms. "I like you, I really do. Let's hope that sister of yours makes the right choice."

She didn't like depending on others for, well, anything, but Ivy knew without a doubt that she needed the women who'd gathered around her. All of them, young and old.

"Helen, what do I need to do next?" What she didn't say was

Help me. Help me please.

Helen opened her mouth to answer, but was interrupted by the ding announcing that someone else was entering the library. All heads turned to see who it was. The Harper brothers tottered toward the front of the library, either too curious to wait or bored by the conversation.

Travis soon joined them. The old men were right behind him.

"What's this?" Travis asked, his eyes widening as he saw the secret library that had been revealed. "I'll be damned." He looked at Marnie. "How long have you been keeping this a secret?"

"Me?" Marnie asked. "Don't look at *me*. This is news to me just like it is to you."

Helen held up a hand to silence everyone. "We need Eve in on this."

"Why?" Ivy asked. "I don't want to do anything that will upset Eve. She's..."

"Oh, dear," Ginger whispered. "We might be too late."

Travis paled. He knew that it was always wise to listen to these sometimes-annoying old women. He turned and ran. Ivy followed. She couldn't keep up with him, but she tried. They ran across the street, only to find the cafe closed. The lights were off, the door was locked. Travis shook the door forcefully, then reached into his pocket for a big set of keys.

"She's going to be ok," Ivy said. "If something was wrong, I'd know it." Wouldn't she?

Travis's hands shook as he unlocked the door. "Five minutes ago she was in the kitchen cooking. Now the place is closed, the door locked? Forgive me if I'm not ready to put every hope I have on your twin's intuition."

He opened the door and ran for the kitchen. While the main room of the cafe was dark, the lights in the kitchen burned bright.

No Eve.

No one at all.

And as they stepped beyond the big stove, they saw what had once been a pot of chicken and dumplings spilled across the floor. Two words had been crudely written in the gravy.

Find Me.

CHAPTER 19

For the first time in her life, Ivy was paralyzed. She didn't know what to do, where to go. Eve was missing, in the hands of the man who'd poisoned Grant.

Eve. The baby she carried. Grant. All were in danger, thanks to her. Levi would've left them alone if not for that stupid book! How the hell had he found it? As far as she knew, he didn't even possess much magic.

Not that he'd shared, with her or with anyone, but she could see now that he'd been wearing a false front. He'd fooled them all.

Travis was in a panic. The laid-back police chief was never rattled, but with Eve missing he was a mess. He loved her; she loved him. They didn't deserve this.

Since Travis was next to worthless, she couldn't be. She couldn't afford to fall apart, not until after this was all over. If there was an after.

Dear God, let there be an after…

"We have to find Levi," she said, grabbing Travis's arm and forcing him to look at her. "He's behind all of this, I don't know why no one saw it sooner."

Felicity and Bria walked into the kitchen, Felicity offering an answer to the question Ivy had just asked. "He was hiding. He still is."

"How do you hide something like this in Mystic Springs?" Ivy snapped.

"With dark power," Bria said.

Neither of them were surprised to find Eve gone, but they both shuddered at the sight of the note that had been left on the floor.

"How can we find him?" Travis asked. "He can't hide from all of us, he can't hide forever. When I get my hands on him..."

"You can have him when Eve and Grant are both safe," Ivy snapped. "He poisoned Grant and probably did the same to Eve. There has to be an antidote, a cure, something. Until we know what he wants..."

"He wants you to choose," Bria said.

Ivy looked to the young girl. *Her choice* was written in the book, but she didn't know what it meant.

And then, with horror, she did. The man she loved or her twin and the child she carried. Would Levi actually make her save one of the people she loved and let the other die?

"There has to be another way."

She thought of the mural that had been taking shape, the figures she'd seen there. Grant at one end of the street, a redhead at the other. She'd thought that redhead by the bakery was her, but maybe it was Eve, and the mural was a symbol, a warning of some kind. A warning she'd missed.

Without telling anyone where she was going, Ivy took off at a run. She wasn't waiting for a bus, and she didn't want to take the time to explain. She flew out of the cafe, turned, and cut sharply around some poor sap who was headed to the cafe for a dinner he wasn't going to get. She moved into the street and ran. A car backing up almost hit her and she screamed at them to get out of her way. Jordan came out of her ice cream shop and stopped to stare.

She heard Travis behind her, then the girls. A glance back showed that the folks from The Egg were getting back on the bus. Marnie was running, too. The librarian wasn't a fan of running, but even she refused to wait for the slowpokes to get back on the bus.

Ivy cut to the other side of the street, past the chocolate shop, and to the clearing in front of the mural.

The painting had changed again.

The stars were brighter, the scene below dimmer. Streetlamps burned softly. The figures that had been there before hadn't changed. Grant by the Egg; Eve in front of the bakery. But a new figure had been added.

In this newest version, another redhead stood in the middle of the street. This time, Ivy knew it was her. The new figure wore a lavender apron, a detail which made identification easy. Her hands were outstretched, and the beginnings of a magical light glowed at her fingertips.

Travis stood behind her. He cursed, then he ran forward and touched the wall. "What the hell is this? Why have I never seen it before?"

"It's been like this for days," Ivy said. "But it keeps changing."

"What does it mean?"

They were both shocked when Ruby walked around the building and joined them. "It means that tonight, no later than midnight, Ivy will have to choose. One will live, the other will die. Levi has a cure, but there's only enough for one. When Ivy makes that choice, whatever it might be, the barrier that traps our magic here will fall."

Travis made a move toward Ruby, but she took a step back and lifted a hand in what looked to be a warning.

"Touch me and Levi will make the choice for you. Might work, might not. If it doesn't work he'll let them both die, along with anyone else who gets in his way. I'm guessing that's a chance you don't want to take."

Ivy pointed to the mural. "This is insane! I don't have that kind of power. I bake and I make amnesia punch the way my mother once did, that's it. That person, whoever she is, has power in her fingertips. I don't!"

"Look again," Ruby said with a grin.

Ivy glanced at the hand she'd lifted to the mural. Her fingertips glowed, as they did in the mural. Not only that, but her hands were warm. They tingled.

She looked to Ruby again. Her heart pounded so hard, she was sure everyone else there could hear it. "Tell Levi I've made my decision."

"Ivy, no," Travis said. "We have time to come up with another solution."

She ignored him. This choice was no choice at all. "Tell Levi that he can have me. Give Eve and Grant both a cure and take me." She was betting that if he had one cure, he either already had or could make another. "If I really do have the power to break the barrier and set his magic free, this is the only way."

"That's not right," one of the girls whispered. She wasn't sure which one.

"I'm meant to choose," Ivy said. "This is it. This is my choice. I choose to sacrifice myself to save the people I love." She gave Ruby her coldest glare. "Take it or leave it."

Levi sat in an uncomfortable chair in the room over the bakery, and watched an unconscious Eve... sleep? Die? He wasn't sure which, but it didn't matter.

Ivy would never think to look for him here.

In a few hours it would be over. Someone would die; someone would live. And he'd leave Mystic Springs with his powers intact. By this time next year he'd be living a life of luxury. He'd be rich and famous; he'd have everything he'd ever wanted. No, it wouldn't take anywhere near a year...

He'd left the back door unlocked for Ruby. He heard her coming up the stairs. Three nights out of the month she could sneak up on anyone without making a sound, but in her human form, the she-wolf didn't exactly have a light step.

"Change of plans," Ruby said as she entered the room. "Ivy doesn't want to pick. She wants you to cure them both and kill her instead."

"I thought she might say something like that. It's tempting, she's been such a pain in my ass, but there's no guarantee that will work."

Ruby perched on his knee. "I hope she saves Eve. I like her, and she's pregnant, and..."

"Don't go soft on me now," he said, pinching her generous backside. "If you have doubts, think of spending the next full moon in Seattle, where you can enjoy the night ripping out the throat of the man who hurt you. You've fantasized about it enough, don't you want to see it become reality?"

"I do." She sighed. "Just saying I hope Ivy chooses to save her twin instead of the jerk who broke her heart."

He didn't care which one died. He didn't care if he left a hundred bodies in his wake as he left Mystic Springs.

"We're almost done with this, just a few more hours to go," Ruby said. "So you can tell me, did you shoot Grant?"

"No."

"So, it was some kind of weird coincidence?"

He smiled. "No."

"Come on, tell me," Ruby said as she turned in his lap and wrapped her arms around his neck. "I'm curious."

"You know, there's a very old saying about curiosity killing the cat. Aren't you afraid the same is true of canines?"

"Very funny." She leaned in and kissed him, but he drew away so that the kiss was a short one.

"This is not the time for fooling around," he said.

"You're nervous. A roll in the hay might help you unwind. Eve won't mind," she whispered as she licked his earlobe.

Ruby had played her part, most recently in taking Eve down and slipping a potion into Grant's food to make sure his memories returned with a vengeance. He'd planted the idea to feed Grant in Travis's head, then had Ruby deliver the special sauce. His she-wolf had been a lot of fun along the way, but he was finished with her. She'd done her part. She thought they'd be leaving town together tonight.

So did Molly.

They were both wrong.

"So, is the mural your work, too?" she asked.

"What mural?"

Eve moaned and squirmed.

"She's waking up," Ruby said. "Is that…"

"Expected?" He finished for her. "Yes. Grant should be coming to as well. It won't hurt Ivy nearly as much to watch an unconscious loved one just slip away. I want her to look her twin and the man she loves in the eye when she sentences one of them to death. I want the decision to hurt. In order for this to work, Ivy really must fall. Hard."

CHAPTER 20

Main Street should be deserted as midnight approached. It usually was, unless there was a festival or a street party, an equinox or solstice.

Tonight Springers were drawn by a power most of them didn't understand. Young and old and in-between they milled along the sidewalks, whispered to one another, watched and waited. An ancient instinct told them something important was coming.

Ivy stood in the middle of the street, where the mural had placed her. There was something mystical about the painting, and while it was hard to know anything for sure, it felt friendly. More helpful than not. Had the mural been a warning? An intended heads up? If so, she'd missed the meaning entirely.

With not much more than fifteen minutes to go until midnight, she saw movement not far from The Egg. A flash of color; a blur. It wasn't long before she realized that was Grant, and he was running toward her. The Egg bus was not far behind him.

Ivy ran to meet him. She'd been sure Levi's poison would keep Grant and Eve both unconscious until the end, but she'd been wrong. Thank God. She could kiss Grant before she left this world. She could tell him, once and for all, how much she loved him. When she saw Travis take off at a run in the other direction, she knew Eve was there, as she'd been in the mural. Alive, for now. Awake and aware.

She couldn't be in two places at once, but even as she ran toward Grant she sent her twin a message. *I love you. Take care of that baby.*

The response was more like something Ivy herself would've said, rather than sweet Eve. *Don't do anything stupid.*

Stupid was all she had left…

Ivy met Grant near the mural. Looking as healthy and alive as ever, he wrapped his arms around her and lifted her off her feet. She didn't mean to cry, she never cried, but tears streamed down her face. Holding him was a joy she'd never thought to experience again.

"I love you," she said. "I love you so much."

"I love you, too," he said. "Helen explained some of what's going on. Where the hell is the bastard? I'm going to…"

"He's not here, but he's coming," she said. She leaned back just enough that she could see his face.

"I feel fine," he said. "More than fine. Whatever he gave me, I think it's worn off. It's a bluff."

"I can't take that chance."

"We'll face him together, if he's fool enough to show up. Just let me get my hands on him."

She kissed him again. No Non-Springer would understand what was happening, not fully. Not even Grant.

"He wants me to choose," she whispered. "I refuse. I won't condemn one of the two people in the world I love to death. Levi can have me, if that's…"

"He can *not*!" Grant snapped. "There has to be another way." He took her face in his hands. "I won't lose you, not again."

The bus came to a stop behind him. The doors whished open,

and in just a couple of minutes Helen Benedict stepped into the street, with the benefit of a cane and the arm of one of the Harper brothers who'd gone to the library with them that afternoon. Tobias had seemed clueless at that time. Now, not so much. He was on guard, doing his best to steady and protect the woman he assisted.

Tobias and his brother had always appeared feeble, to Ivy. A little lost. A bit confused. At the moment Tobias looked like a man on a mission. A soldier. A knight.

"There is another way," Helen said as she and her friend approached. "I think."

Levi waited until it was almost midnight. For effect, for drama. And because, frankly, he enjoyed the anticipation. He was euphoric.

Everything was as he'd planned. Eve and Travis were together, holding one another closely not far from the police station where Travis spent most of his days. Ivy and Grant stood in the middle of the street, not clutching one another in quite the same way, but holding hands and looking solemn. Ivy had been crying.

Good.

His ego resented the fact that she'd so easily brushed him off for the past several months. That made torturing her much easier, much more enjoyable. The pain would make her fall all the more sweet, and perhaps more powerful, as well.

He'd realized some Springers would be drawn to Main Street by the energy that had been created here tonight, but he hadn't expected quite so many. All the Benedicts. Silas and Gabi, with a kid in a stroller. This was no place for a child, even he knew that. A bunch of old folks from The Egg had gathered not far from Ivy, and so had a few teenagers.

The old folks looked surprisingly fierce, but they couldn't help Ivy now. No one could.

Molly and Ruby were present, too. They weren't together, but both stood near the ice cream shop.

"Have you made your choice?" he asked as he walked toward Ivy.

"I have," she said, her voice stronger than he'd expected it would be. "As you know, since I sent a message with your friend, Ruby, I choose myself. Take me. Let Eve and Grant both live."

Grant protested, but Ivy ignored him.

Levi shook his head. "That's not how it works, dearie. Your husband or your sister. Which one will survive this night?"

Helen Benedict, the interfering biddy, stepped between him and his prey, between him and what he'd wanted and planned for so long. "I never liked you," she said, pursing her thin lips.

"The feeling is mutual." She was one of those he'd never been able to penetrate, never been able to influence. Peeking into her gray head was impossible, even now.

If he had more time he'd take care of her here and now, along with a few other annoying Springers.

"We have a few minutes, Levi," she said. "Maybe you can answer a few questions for me?"

"Why should I?"

"Why not, sonny? You hold all the cards here, why not share a hint of your brilliance?"

She was being sarcastic, but... she wasn't wrong. "Fine. Fire away, while there's still time."

"My first question is, who brought Grant back to us?"

He smiled. "A couple of very powerful girls who are not as resistant to my powers as you are."

The girls in question, Bria and Felicity, gasped. Both of them. He looked their way. "You're young. Don't feel bad that there are still a few glitches in your abilities."

One of the girls whispered, "I don't have glitches."

The other looked at the asphalt beneath her feet.

"Who shot Grant?" Helen continued. "Was that you?"

He started to deny involvement, but why bother? This was almost over. Why not take credit for all his hard work? "Not directly. A friend took on the chore for me."

He realized he should've kept his mouth shut when Molly jogged toward him. "I'm more than a friend," she said defensively. "Levi loves me and I love him. I know this plan of his seems unnecessarily harsh, but in the end the sacrifices made here tonight will pay off for all of you who will be left behind."

Levi sighed. He heard as well as felt Ruby follow Molly onto the street. "You?" his she-wolf snapped. "What makes you think Levi loves *you*?"

"We've been together for months," Molly said.

"Months!"

Was that a growl?

Levi turned to face the two women. He didn't have the energy to spare, and he was so excited about what was to come that harnessing his power wouldn't be easy, but he could calm Molly easily enough. She was weak-minded. Ruby was another matter, but she too could be handled.

"Ladies," he said in his most charming voice. "I love you both so much, and I appreciate all you've done." He cast a calming shield over Molly, and she deflated a bit. But Ruby… Ruby had never been that easy.

What came next happened fast, much too fast. The light that filled the sky above was unnatural. He knew where it was coming from; Ivy Franklin, the woman at the center of it all, the core of the power that could free him, and so many others. Some in the crowd shielded their eyes against the brightness. He did not, so Ivy's light illuminated what was coming for him all too well.

Ruby was shifting. There was no full moon, the time wasn't right, but with that powerful light that was emanating from Ivy, his she-wolf was transformed.

He started to try to reason with her, but didn't manage a single word before her claws flew toward his throat and slashed into his flesh.

Levi fell to the street hard, landing on his back so he was staring up at the sky. The stars there were perfectly aligned. The barrier that had trapped incredible power here for years began to crumble. Did no one else see it? Was the view only for him? There was no time to enjoy the sight. He felt his life slipping away, felt his own blood leaving his body far too quickly. There were no images of his life, as he'd heard there might be, no tunnel of light he might follow into the afterlife.

Ivy stood over him, her glowing hands lifted to the night sky, the light she created traveling upward with such force it was sure to break the barrier completely, if it hadn't already.

Just as he'd dreamed of. Freedom from this place, from this life.

Molly and Ruby—fully human again—glared down at him. He was dying, and dying quickly. These women who'd claimed to love him watched without any evidence of sorrow.

Mere minutes before midnight, Levi glanced up one last time.

Though things hadn't gone as planned, the spell had worked. He'd realized someone would be sacrificed tonight, but he'd never imagined it would be him.

He saw Ivy's light rising up, drifting this way and that, growing stronger. It was almost… beautiful. That light was going to punch through what remained of the barrier above to spread far and wide. The people of Mystic Springs were free, but he would not be joining them in discovering the joys and the pitfalls of a new way of living.

Levi wondered if Eve and Grant would both die now, without the vial, the cure he carried in his pocket.

He hoped so. His last thought was one of revenge.

~

Grant caught Ivy as she fell. Whatever had happened, whatever power she'd loosed through her hands, had depleted her.

All around him people talked too loudly and asked questions he couldn't answer. A few bent over Redmon. Travis really should be arresting Ruby, the woman who'd ripped out the doctor's throat, but he was focused entirely on his wife.

Half a block away, a woman screamed and drew his attention. A very pregnant woman shouted, "My water broke!"

A handful of women headed toward the mother-to-be, smiles on their faces. Drama and death one minute; new life the next. Wasn't that the way of the world? A nurse he recognized from his time at The Egg yelled, "Bring Cindy to the doctor's office! Break in, if you have to. I don't think she'll make it to Eufaula."

No one questioned that statement.

A woman burst forward. "I have a spare key. No need to break in."

Ivy opened her eyes. "You're okay," she whispered. She smiled, and then she didn't. "Eve!" She tried to sit up, but was too weak to do it without his help. Sitting in the middle of Main Street, he held her close.

"Eve is fine." For now. Would they both die? In minutes, in hours, as the sun rose…

Felicity and her friend ran to Redmon's body. They really shouldn't be exposed to that kind of horror, but they were here and had witnessed the doctor's murder, like everyone else who milled the streets in the middle of the night. Even though they ran to the body, not away, both girls were obviously squeamish. It was a gruesome sight.

"The medicine is in his pocket," Felicity said. "I don't know how much time we have, but I'm thinking not much."

It was Molly who knelt by the body and bravely reached into one pocket and then another. "I don't know what I was thinking," she said, sounding confused. "Levi was…" She shuddered. "He was inside me, in my head all the time. I did terrible things. I remember, but I don't know why I did them."

Molly found the vial she was looking for, grasped it in her hand, and stood tall. "There's just one, and I don't think it's enough for both. I don't understand how I know, but… how can we be sure?" She placed her free hand on the young girl before her, searching for guidance from children.

Powerful children.

"I have an idea," Bria said. There was a touch of hope in her voice, a light that gave Grant hope of his own. She whispered to Felicity, then the two girls ran to Helen and her friends.

Was his life in the hands of teenagers and residents of the old folks' home? It sure looked that way, as the five females formed a circle. It was Ginger who held the vial in her hand as the women chanted, looked to the sky, and created their own light. That unnatural light was blue and green, and it sparkled.

Sparkled and then coalesced in Ginger's hand.

Two old men who'd been hanging around lately seemed to shift and change. For a moment, just a moment, they appeared to be younger and stronger. They were dressed in some kind of shimmering armor that was more illusion than real. They were knights guarding their women, keeping them safe in unsafe times.

Ginger lifted her hand high, and instead of one vial there were now two.

Bria took one vial and ran to Eve and Travis.

Felicity ran to him. "Drink this," she ordered.

He took the vial with more than a little suspicion. "Are you sure it's safe?"

"Yes?" she said, but she didn't sound entirely certain. "Yes," she said again with a bit more confidence.

Grant looked toward Eve and Travis, as Ivy's twin put her vial to her mouth and drank every drop.

Well hell, if it was good enough for Eve…

Grant drank the vile potion. It burned a little as it went down. It tasted like licorice and, dammit, cabbage.

He didn't feel any different after ingesting the potion, but Felicity placed a hand on his shoulder and smiled. "You're going to be okay."

Given everything that had happened tonight, *okay* seemed like a stretch.

Ivy raised up and placed her head on his shoulder. "We can trust Felicity," she said, still too weak. "She's one of a kind." Then she smiled.

Grant said the first thing that came to his mind. "Marry me."

Ivy smiled; that smile was still too weak for his liking. "We're already married."

"Marry me again. I want a real wedding this time, with your friends and mine in attendance. I want my parents to be there."

Ivy screwed up her nose. "They won't like me."

"They'll love you."

"I'm not all that lovable."

He kissed her to stop her arguing, and because he couldn't wait another minute.

Her energy must be coming back; she returned the kiss with an appropriate amount of vigor.

"Is that a no?" he asked when the kiss was done.

Ivy sighed. "Look around you. This is my world, and it's not always an easy one. If you stay, if we make a life here, it will be your world, too."

He glanced up, as she'd asked him to. She'd told him there was magic here and he'd accepted it. Until now, he hadn't seen much evidence of what made Mystic Springs what it was.

Just feet away, a toddler in a stroller was talking to a bloodhound. The bloodhound seemed to talk back, in a language only the two of them understood.

A pretty blonde—he'd seen her in the ice cream shop—lifted her hand. He followed her gaze up and saw that she seemed to be directing clouds away from the center of town. It was raining to the north and to the south, but it wasn't raining *here*.

A middle-aged woman waved her hand over the area where Redmon's body had been a few minutes earlier. The blood that had stained the street disappeared. A young man provided an unnatural light for her work, using nothing but his hands.

At the end of the street, just this side of the rain, stood the librarian. She held her very young child in her arms. Next to her stood... Bigfoot. Seven feet tall, hairy as hell, not a man nor an ape but... Bigfoot. The creature held out a hand, and the baby clutched a hairy finger.

Just a few feet away, Helen and her friends cackled. There was no other word for it. One of them said, "Girls, we've still got it."

He wasn't sure what *it* was, but whatever it was made the older women look younger. Stronger. They... glowed.

"It is different," he said.

"You have no idea how different. I won't make you stay; I won't do that to you," Ivy whispered.

Grant smiled down at her. The decision he had to make was an easy one. He wasn't giving up his wife, not ever again. "You can't make me leave."

"Actually I..."

He leaned in and down and kissed her again. "You can't make me leave. No matter what happens, I will always find my way back to you."

Ivy sighed, long and slow, and it seemed the expression on her face changed subtly. Gone was the last hint of uncertainty, the final speck of anger. "I'll marry you again. Be warned, husband. This time... this time I'm going to hold on to you with everything I've got."

CHAPTER 21

Ivy had considered having the wedding on Halloween, but she didn't really want all their anniversaries from now until the end of time to be littered with plastic spiders and fake cobwebs and little kids on a sugar high. The first weekend in November had turned out to be perfect, for everyone.

The weather was too cool for her yellow sundress, so she'd chosen a traditional but simple white gown and would carry yellow roses. Eve would be her matron of honor. Grant's dad was going to stand up with him, serving as best man.

She'd made her own wedding cake that morning. Who else could she trust with that important task?

It had been an eventful couple of weeks. Two days after Ruby had killed Levi, three of the five Milhouse boys left Mystic Springs to find their cousin. The Milhouses weren't always the best of men, they were all too often rude and crude. But they weren't murderers, and they considered it their responsibility to stop Ruby, if they could. How? No one had asked...

The psychics in town had varying opinions about whether or not the barrier around Mystic Springs had been breached that night. *Something* had happened, they all agreed on that, but that was where the agreement ended. There hadn't been news about people outside Mystic Springs developing powers. Maybe it would take some time, if that was the case. Then again, maybe the magic that had been contained in Mystic Springs had simply dissipated. Maybe it had never been as powerful as they'd believed. Perhaps the barrier had broken and then healed itself.

They'd find out soon enough, since tomorrow night would be the first full moon since the event. Some individual magics could be hidden. They might develop slowly, over time. But if werewolves made an appearance outside Mystic Springs, everyone would know.

The mural remained a mystery. Ivy had been certain the creator was either one of the old ladies from The Egg, or else Felicity and Bria. Who else would have the power to create something like that? They all denied responsibility, and at this point, why would they lie? More than one Springer had decided to camp out all night and wait for the mural to change, but they always fell asleep before anything happened and woke to see that there was a new section, or a shift in the scene.

At the moment, her wedding was displayed on the mural. As usual it was imperfect, but she and Grant were clear as day, as were the yellow roses and a lot of wedding guests. Too many guests, to be honest.

As the time approached, Ivy had second thoughts. Not about Grant, never about Grant. They should've gotten married *again* away from Mystic Springs—anywhere but here—but it was too late for that. Numerous folding chairs were set up in the street, behind the altar that was decorated with fall leaves and a long garland sporting more yellow flowers. Her friends and Grant's milled around the downtown area and filled the chairs. As was usual for many of the town's events, there were refreshments on tables that had been set up on the sidewalk.

She'd never seen so many Non-Springers on Main Street, not all at once. Baseball players and their wives, Grant's family, even his agent! And not a one of them had had any trouble finding their way here. That in itself was strange.

Like everything else about her life was strange.

One of the guests had riled her at first glance. The second baseman who'd all but crippled Grant was in attendance. He was a friend? Grant said the accident hadn't been intentional or personal, but Ivy kept thinking of potions she might slip into the jerk's punch. Something mostly innocuous. Mostly. Grant convinced her to let it go.

She'd never been particularly good at letting things go.

Ivy hated being the center of attention. But for this one day, her second wedding day, she didn't mind nearly as much as she'd thought she would. She wanted the world to know how much she loved her husband.

She'd been in the bakery since sunrise, baking as she always did when she was nervous. In just a few minutes she'd go upstairs and put on her wedding dress, fix her makeup—again—and fiddle with her hair. Eve and Marnie would both be there to help.

Grant had been relegated to the B&B, along with his parents, his agent, and those baseball players who'd arrived a day early. Including the jerk. Molly, free of Levi's influence, had been the perfect hostess. No one bothered to tell the out-of-towners that the B&B owner had shot the man they'd come to town to see married. Even though Ivy and Grant had been living together for weeks, and they were, after all, already married, Eve had insisted that they spend the final night before the wedding in separate bedrooms. Something about stupid tradition.

One night, and she missed him already.

Grant's agent Oscar Vernon, a slick little man she'd met last night at the rehearsal dinner, pushed his way into the bakery. Shoot. She hadn't locked the front door! Oscar was short, thin, and mostly bald. Why did he bother to hang onto the few strands of hair he had left? It wasn't an attractive look; entirely bald would be a definite improvement. His suit fit him perfectly, and his shoes were unnaturally shiny. And pointed.

She'd disliked him on sight.

"Sorry, we're closed," she said. "I was just about to…"

"Explain something to me," Oscar said with a wave of one long finger. "Why would a man turn down millions of dollars to play a game he loves in order to stay…" He glanced around her place with undisguised disdain, "Here?"

"What are you talking about?" she asked, her heart flipping over.

"I got a phone call last night, with a fantastic offer for Grant. Maybe he's not as quick as he once was, but he's still a helluva player and there are plenty of teams who see that. I was so excited to tell him about the offer, I asked the woman at the B&B if she had any champagne so we could celebrate. Not only was there no champagne, Grant said he wasn't interested." The man pulled at what little hair he had. "Not interested? What the hell?"

How many times had she told Grant that she wouldn't leave Mystic Springs? Wasn't that why she'd chosen amnesia punch for him five years ago? He'd had to leave. She couldn't. All that she was, all that she would ever be, was here.

Wasn't it?

"Have you told the team he turned down the offer?"

Oscar seemed to deflate. "I was about to do that, but I wanted to have some reason first, something to tell them that makes sense."

"Hold off on that call," she said.

Oscar arched one eyebrow. How did he do that? "Are you telling me…?"

"Just relax, enjoy the wedding, and we'll talk later. Right now, I have to go make myself beautiful for my husband."

With a smarmy smile, he said, "I'm sure that's never an issue."

"Don't push your luck, Oscar."

His bride was even more beautiful than she'd been the first time around. He hadn't thought that to be possible. Ivy walked toward him far too slowly. He wanted her to run; he wanted to run to her. They'd waited long enough for this moment.

The Springers had been on their best behavior, with so many Non-Springers in town. He hadn't seen a hint of magic in the past three days, since the first guest had arrived. He was pretty sure someone other than Eve had prepared the rehearsal dinner meal, because no one had broken down and cried, or found themselves overly sentimental, or gotten caught up in too many tales of times gone by. Just as well.

When Oscar had brought him the offer last night, he hadn't thought twice about turning it down. Everyone had been surprised. His dad had cursed, for the first time ever that Grant knew of. His mom seemed to understand. His brothers and his agent had not. He hadn't even bothered to call Ivy and tell her, because it was a non-starter. He wanted to be wherever she was, and she wanted—needed—to be here.

Travis's brother Luke, who owned the hardware store, performed the ceremony. Apparently he had all the right paperwork, not that it mattered since he and Ivy were already married. This was all for show.

And what a show it was.

Luke said the proper words to get the ball rolling. Grant barely heard them. Then it came time for their vows. He'd been surprised when Ivy insisted that they write their own, given how withdrawn she could be at times, but he would give her whatever she wanted, now and forever.

"I had planned to say something different today," she said, "but as we all know the only constant in life is change. A little while ago, I had to toss out what I'd prepared." She looked him in the eye. "Until I met you, I didn't know what love was. Then for a while I thought I did know, but I was wrong. So very wrong. I believed that love could be recreated, that if you loved one man it would be easy enough to learn to love another, but that's not true. You're it for me, Grant Whitlock. You're my one and only. My life. My own special magic."

She glanced into the crowd of guests, but he couldn't tell who she was looking at, not exactly.

"You've agreed to be a part of my world, because you know how important it is to me. But as I said, everything changes." She shifted her head and looked into his eyes again. "I want to be a part of your world now. It's time."

His heart almost came through his chest. Who'd told her? What was she doing?

"I want to go where you go, husband," she continued. "I want to watch you live your dream, and more, I want to be a part of it. My world will be waiting for us, when the time comes."

It was his turn to speak, and even though he'd rehearsed his vows a hundred times, he found himself speechless.

"Are you saying what I think you're saying?"

"Let's go," she whispered.

He picked her up and swung her around, laughing. She laughed, too. Out of the corner of his eye, he saw Oscar stand up and shake his fists in the air, in a jubilant expression of relief and joy. Someone grabbed the agent's suit jacket and pulled him back down.

"Uh, we're not done," Luke said.

Grant put Ivy on her feet. "I love you," he said, loud enough for everyone to hear. "Now and forever, it's the two of us against the world."

Ivy bit her bottom lip, then held up three fingers and whispered. "Well, the three of us. If I've got this figured right, I'll have this baby during the All-Star break."

Baby. He shouldn't be shocked, but he was. Not so much that Ivy was pregnant, that he was going to be a father, but because she shared the news now, in this very public way. He grinned. "Ivy Whitlock, you're making a spectacle of yourself."

"I suppose I am. I just found out with one of those home tests, and... I couldn't wait to tell you."

Luke smiled and sighed, then said, "In the interest of expediency, I now declare you man and wife. You may..."

Grant didn't wait to be given permission. He kissed his wife well.

The reception was winding down when Ivy took Grant's hand and they walked to the end of the street. She wanted to check out the mural to see what, if anything, had changed.

She should be terrified to even imagine leaving Mystic Springs. She'd been so dead set against it. But once the decision had been made, she was at peace. How often in her life had she really known peace? They had several months before Grant had to report to his new team, and they'd spend those months here, preparing. He'd be getting in shape for another season. She'd be getting herself ready for... for what? New places and new people. A life with the man she loved. A baby.

Babies and change. Just a month ago, hadn't she been bemoaning both?

Sure enough, the mural had shifted. Instead of the wedding that had been depicted this morning, the scene was of falling leaves on Main Street. The sky was gray, as if it were dawn or dusk. Ribbons of light rose from the center of the street and spread in several directions.

She recognized those lights. They'd come from her own hands, on the night Levi had died.

In one of the streams of light, there was what looked to be a crudely drawn baseball being chased by a cupcake. In another a dog raced alongside a child. In yet another, a much older Felicity danced on a beach.

"Does this mean..." Ivy whispered.

"I don't have any idea," Grant whispered before she could finish her sentence. He grabbed her hand, threaded his fingers through hers.

They both heard Gabi calling her daughter's name. Footsteps grew closer, louder. A child laughed. Was there anything more exhilarating than a toddler's laughter? Mia was not just walking, these days, she could run like the wind, and often did. She was also an expert at escaping from her stroller. Basically, the little girl who would turn two next month had the run of the town.

"Come back here!" Gabi called.

Mia rounded the corner, spotted Ivy and Grant, and laughed. Gabi was right behind her daughter, and behind her, Silas and the bloodhound Judge.

They all answered to Mia's whims, at least for now.

Mia squealed, turned to the mural, and spread her arms wide.

The mural shimmered, and the streams of light that had been painted there glowed brightly. The paint changed, shifted.

Mia? She'd tried to guess who was behind the mural, but the toddler had never crossed her mind as a possible suspect. Ivy stared down at the little girl, then back to Gabi and Silas.

"Did you know she was doing this?" Ivy asked.

Both shook their heads. "No idea," Gabi said. "Maybe it's not her, maybe it's..." The words died slowly. Obviously it was Mia "painting" the mural. She saw what was to come and displayed it for the town to see.

More change. More evidence of power.

Mia's arms dropped and she sighed, then laughed again. Silas and Gabi studied the new mural, and Silas sighed loudly. "Looks like we're having a Christmas wedding," he said.

"*Judge* is going to be your best man?" Gabi asked as she studied the scene before them.

"Looks that way."

Ivy and Grant backed away, still holding hands. They left the little family studying the depiction of what was to come for them. A wedding in front of the town Christmas tree, with a light snow falling and Christmas lights twinkling.

And above their heads, streams of light that had once been trapped escaping into the world, not in a flood but in a trickle.

At least for now.

Hand in hand, they walked back toward their wedding reception. Everyone was having a good time. The weather was lovely. The player that had almost crippled Grant was dancing with the woman who owned the new chocolate shop. He looked far too happy.

"I can't believe you won't let me poison him."

"He's on my new team," Grant said. "We need him healthy."

"Just a little barely effective minorly venomous..."

In the middle of the street, her husband turned her around and kissed her properly. Deeply, sweetly, completely. In that moment all was well and she had no desire to poison anyone. Not even the jerk.

"Fine," she said when the kiss was done. "No one will get poisoned today."

"Or tomorrow," Grant said as they resumed their slow walk back toward the crowd.

"Or tomorrow," she conceded. "Oh my God, you want me to forgive him."

"Can you?" Grant asked.

Forgiveness had never been a part of her makeup. She didn't let things go. She didn't turn the other cheek. But at this moment she was so happy, forgiveness seemed... possible.

"He's forgiven, but I swear, if he hurts you again he's fair game."

"Agreed."

Whether she had magic in the outside world or not, she would forever protect the man she loved.

Her life would never be the same. Maybe change wasn't so bad after all…

EPILOGUE

Seattle, Washington

She'd been watching the house for almost a week, waiting. Waiting for the full moon to arrive. Would she shift, as she always had in Mystic Springs? Would she be able to make her dreams come true? Tonight maybe, or sometime during the next two nights. If Levi's plan had worked…

On the night she'd killed Levi, there had been no full moon and yet she'd still been able to shift. That might've been an anomaly brought on by the magic in the air, by the unnatural light Ivy had created, or by Ruby's own emotion. She'd tried several times since to recreate that moment, to change at her own direction without the assistance of the moon.

It hadn't worked. She'd convinced herself that she might have to be satisfied with being a she-wolf three nights out of the month.

The man who'd spurned her wasn't the only one she had a grievance against. Ruby made a mental list. Devin first, then the woman he'd chosen over her, then that bitch from high school, then... so many more. What better way to settle all the old grievances than terror and bloodshed?

There had been a time when she'd had a choice. She might've stayed in Mystic Springs, taken over the cafe when Eve decided to retire and have kids, or else started her own business. She could've played nice, started a new life, let bygones be bygones. But the choice had been made. She was who she was and she couldn't go back. Well, not yet.

One day she'd go back to Mystic Springs and tear Molly Duncan to pieces. This was all her fault, after all. Mousy, weak thing.

She hunkered down behind an overgrown bush and waited for the sun to set and the moon to rise. Finally, it was time.

Nothing happened. Maybe Levi's plan hadn't worked. His death might not have been enough to set things into motion, in spite of the events of that night. Ivy's light; the shift in the universe. Something had changed that night, but was it enough?

Ivy had to be destroyed, Levi had said. She had to *fall*. Had she fallen? Was Levi Redmon any different from any other lying man?

Ruby had to consider that maybe she was an ordinary woman once again, away from Mystic Springs. She was prepared for that, had always known it was possible. Being without magic wouldn't stop her. It wasn't what she wanted, it made her task more dangerous. She rested an anxious hand over the knife she wore at her waist. One way or another...

An hour after dark had fully fallen, a soft rain began to fall. Ruby didn't particularly like the rain, she hated being wet, but the weather wasn't going to deter her. She could rush into the house and take care of business but she waited, wondering if it was still possible that she might shift, wondering how she should proceed if she didn't. She'd almost given up, but another hour or so later, a familiar itch began. She smiled and began to undress. Shoes, socks, jeans, t-shirt and bra. They were all cast aside moments before she changed.

His aroma was sharp, after the change was complete. Devin was still inside the house, but she could smell him as if his flesh was pressed against her snout.

The she-wolf crept to the back door of the modest house she'd once thought might be hers, one day. When Devin married her, when she was his wife. Instead he'd been screwing around all along and had chosen the other one.

She wasn't the kind of woman he wanted to take home to Mother.

What would Mother say now? Ruby added Mother to her mental list.

The back doorknob rattled, then swung open. Devin stepped onto the patio carrying a bag of garbage. She took some comfort in the fact that he didn't look happy, as he walked toward the garbage can a few feet from the back door.

"Take out the garbage, fix the sink, why are your socks on the floor?" he mumbled as he opened the bin and tossed the bag inside.

Ruby sprung, intent on Devin's throat. He was vulnerable there, as all men were. He'd be dead in seconds and then she'd feed on his entrails. When that bitch of a wife came out to see where her husband had gone she'd kill her, too…

She didn't see or hear the others coming. One of them reached her just before her dream came true. One talon scratched Devin's throat, before she was knocked away and went rolling across the grass.

Devin screamed and bolted for the back door. Ruby jumped up, onto all fours; she heard the back door slam and the lock engage.

She faced three of her own kind. Cousins? Probably. How the hell had they found her? Scent, most likely. It was powerful.

Maybe it was more than that. Had she told anyone she was headed to Seattle?

Only Levi, and he was dead. Who would he have told? No one. He'd hidden his true self too well for gossip and confessions.

No one had told anything. There were too damn many psychics in Mystic Springs.

The others spread out, effectively surrounding her. She could fight one of them, she could beat one, but three?

Ruby tried to shift back to her human form, hoping that her powers were different enough in this new world that she could manage. The boys wouldn't hurt her if she was a defenseless woman. They wouldn't dare.

She couldn't make herself change. If she had a voice she'd argue that she was a cousin. A distant one, but still, family. You don't murder family! She'd also argue that Devin needed to die, that she was justified. But she had no voice.

One of the wolves pounced; she was almost positive that was Donnie. Figures it would be him. He was the biggest asshole of the bunch. The other two moved in, growling. The one with red hair had to be Weston. She wasn't sure about the third cousin. There were so damn many of them.

Donnie used his claws on her throat without hesitation. Blood poured, pain radiated through her body. She wondered briefly if her cousins would devour her when she was dead. It wasn't their way, but then it hadn't been hers until now.

Not a single tooth touched her, but it's not like teeth were necessary. Blood gushed from the wound at her throat. She'd be dead soon enough.

The full moon overhead was bright and beautiful. The rain stopped, and the big moon peeked through thin clouds. It illuminated Ruby as her she-wolf form was replaced with vulnerable, damaged flesh. Her cousins departed, their work done.

Maybe they'd blame Devin for her murder. Maybe he'd go to

prison for the rest of his miserable life. That wasn't much, but it was something to hold onto as she died.

~

In a diner in Oklahoma, three hairy brothers ate eggs and pancakes as if they hadn't had a meal in days. The truth was, they'd eaten just fine in the days since they'd dispatched Ruby.

A she-wolf on a rampage wasn't good for werewolf PR.

They'd stayed in Seattle for another two nights after the deed was done, wondering how journalists might explain away a naked woman with her throat all but torn out. They'd kept waiting for an uproar, but the story had barely been a blip on the local evening news. There hadn't been much to speak of in the newspaper.

During those two nights both Donnie and Tyler had shifted, as usual, but Weston had been able to avoid the change. Not that he didn't enjoy being who he was, he'd just wanted to see if he could hold back. He had.

"We can be home tonight," Weston said between big bites of a fluffy pancake.

"Or we can travel a while longer, see what the world holds for us," Donnie argued. "We're not tied to Mystic Springs, not anymore."

"Dad will kick your ass if you don't come home," Tyler said as he signaled the busy waitress for more coffee.

"He can try," Donnie said, and then they all laughed. Harry Milhouse might be getting older, but he was still tough as nails and capable of kicking all their asses, if it suited him.

The waitress refilled their coffee cups and moved on as quickly as possible.

Weston patted his jacket pocket. "We've done what we set out to do, and we have the proof." The newspaper clipping was wildly wrong, but it did name Ruby as the victim of an animal attack.

Coyote, wild dog, mountain lion, no one knew what kind of animal.

No one had surmised werewolf. Too bad. *Werewolf in Seattle* would make a kickass headline.

Weston did wonder what the intended victim's wife had to say about an ex-girlfriend being found naked and dead in the back yard. That would be tough to explain away. Fortunately, the truth wasn't likely to occur to anyone.

Not unless there were a lot more distant cousins in the real world and they started to change during the full moons to come. Then, maybe...

They could go anywhere, live wherever they wanted to and shift when the moon was full. If they got tired of that new place, they could more to another. The world was wide open to them now.

But Mystic Springs was home. It would always be home. They belonged there and always would. None of them wanted to live anywhere else. Besides, the band got the occasional gig in Eufaula, and it wouldn't be the same without all five of the brothers. They were pretty good, if he did say so himself.

Donnie paid, and Tyler added to the tip. Donnie was notoriously cheap.

In the parking lot, standing by their pickup truck, they each took a long look around. By tonight they'd be back home, which is where they needed to be, but that didn't mean that the world beyond Mystic Springs didn't hold any appeal.

It was Saturday morning, and kids were playing soccer in a field across the street from the diner. They laughed and screamed and kicked the ball. Some of them were good at the sport. Others were not. They all seemed to be having a good time.

Weston had been keeping an eye out for signs of Mystic Springs magic in the real world. He'd seen lots of weird shit, that was for sure, but magic? None.

Until now.

One of the kids kicked the soccer ball toward the net. It looked as if it was headed straight in, hard and accurate. Feet from the goalie, who was standing in the middle of the goal with his hands up and ready, the ball took a sharp turn in mid-air. It didn't just miss the mark, it went wildly off course.

"Huh," Tyler said. He'd been watching, too.

"What do you think?" Weston asked.

"I think that kid is going to be one hell of a goalie."

All three of them laughed as they climbed into the truck. It was Donnie's turn to drive. Weston, delegated to the back seat since he was the youngest, watched the game as they drove away. The players and parents apparently didn't give the misbehaving ball a second thought. No one examined it. No one looked puzzled. They just resumed play.

But Weston knew, the real world was about the change in a big way. For the better?

Only time would tell.

The End

ABOUT THE AUTHOR

Linda's first book, the historical romance *Guardian Angel,* was released in 1994, and in the years since she's written in several romance sub-genres under several names. In order of appearance, Linda Winstead; Linda Jones; Linda Winstead Jones; Linda Devlin; and Linda Fallon. She's a six time finalist for the RITA Award and a winner (for *Shades of Midnight*) in the paranormal category. She's a New York Times and USA Today bestselling author of more than seventy books. Most recently she's been writing as Linda Jones in a couple of joint projects with Linda Howard, re-releasing some of her backlist in e-book format, and diving into a new paranormal series set in the fictional Alabama town of Mystic Springs.

Sign up for Linda's newsletter at her website.

www.lindawinsteadjones.com
lindawinsteadjonesauthor@gmail.com

ALSO BY LINDA WINSTEAD JONES

Mystic Springs

Bigfoot and the Librarian

Santa and the Snow Witch, a novella

Beauty and the Beastmaster

Ivy's Fall

Sinclair Undercover

Hot On His Trail

Capturing Cleo

In Bed With Boone

Clint's Wild Ride

On Dean's Watch

Last Chance Heroes

Running Scared

Truly, Madly, Dangerously

One Major Distraction

Lucky's Woman

The Guardian

Fantasy/Paranormal

The Sun Witch

The Moon Witch

The Star Witch

For more, visit Linda's website at www.lindawinsteadjones.com

Made in the USA
Las Vegas, NV
16 July 2022

51615221R10105